# Do you
# remember
# Paris?

# Do you remember Paris?

How could I forget

## MELANIE ELIZABETH INGRAM

POPLAR MYSTERIES

ISBN 978-1-7390268-0-6

**Book Disclaimer**

This book is a work of fiction created solely for entertainment purposes.
Any resemblance to actual people, living or deceased, or to real-life
events, is purely coincidental. All characters, timelines, and incidents in
this book are products of the author's imagination.

To Georgia, Max, and Alex
The Intrepid Three Musketeers
With Love, this book is dedicated to you.

Auntie Melanie

xxx

# Contents

# 1

## No Ordinary Day

### October 30, 2009

Charlie walked over to his desk, opened a drawer, and reached for his cigarettes and lighter. Yes, he had promised to give up, but today was not that day. A doctor never wants to hear that their patient has just been found dead, let alone washed up alongside the docks, found by a passing dog-walker. As he paced towards the window and lit his cigarette, he kept asking himself what had gone wrong. As a consultant psychiatrist, what had he missed? He had seen Emily just one day ago and been happy to discharge her to continue as an outpatient.

Opening the window, he felt a gush of cool evening air on his face. He listened to the pounding rain splashing on the windowsill, and the familiar sound of rush-hour traffic. The city lights twinkled and seemed magical on the horizon. Suddenly, Charlie's thoughts were interrupted by a familiar tap at the door. Rachael, his personal assistant, entered holding a newspaper neatly folded in half. She held it out.

1

"I brought you the evening edition and, well," Rachael paused, "I think you should see this. They're all over it, I'm afraid. The phone has not stopped. I managed to put off a lot of the calls. However, the coroner's office called to say they'll be in touch when the autopsy report is complete. The police are starting their investigation. Detective Jane Wyatt is in charge and asked you to return her call. I have her details written down here."

Charlie took the newspaper and placed it on his desk, thanking Rachael for her help. He just wanted to be alone when he read the headlines. "Well," she said, "I'll leave you to it. I just want to confirm next week's appointments before I go." As Rachael was about to leave, she turned around. "Oh, before I forget, your wife called. Can you call her back and discuss Lilly's birthday party?" Charlie nodded. Delores lived in her own little socialite world. Organising their daughter's eighteenth was all she talked about, and he knew the guest list would be endless, the arrangements a melodrama.

Charlie sat down and carefully unfolded the newspaper. He felt cold and unable to move as he read the headline.

*Woman Found Washed Up on Canal Side*
*Practised Witchcraft, Say Locals*

Beneath was a picture of Emily. Her deep brown eyes were staring out at him, and the pendant she always wore seemed to be gleaming.

2

**NEWS**

**Woman Found Washed Up on Canal Side**

PRACTISED WITCHCRAFT, SAY LOCALS

As he continued to read, his mind drifted back to the last time he had seen her. Her words were now haunting him. At the end of a long consultation, he had asked whether she remembered the first time she had experienced clairvoyant ability. Emily had tilted her head to the side and smiled. "Since I was a child," she answered. "May I now ask you a question?" He had nodded. "Do you remember Paris? The woman that you loved and then left. She will never forget. I know you will meet her again. However, it will be when you are least expecting it."

Although shocked by Emily's revelation, Charlie had remained calm and smiled.

"That's an interesting speculation, Emily," he answered. "Our time is up for today. Perhaps we could continue with those thoughts next time."

Emily nodded and then stood up, ready to leave.

"Goodbye, Dr. Ferguson. Until we meet again." She then paused for a moment. "Or perhaps we won't." Before he could reply, she was out the door.

How could Emily have known? Twenty years ago, he had fallen in love with Sophie, the girl he adored and had wanted to be with.

There was a flickering of light, and Charlie heard an unusually loud slam of what seemed to be the door to Rachael's office. He opened his door to investigate.

"Rachael, are you ok?" he called. Entering her room, he stood in disbelief. The filing cabinet drawers were wide open, papers were strewn across the floor, and the folder that had contained Emily's file lay empty in the wastepaper bin. Clearly it had been stolen.

Not wanting to touch anything, he raced back to his desk and rang for the police. Then he descended to the lobby to check with the concierge at the reception desk. Rachael had left the building as usual. However, a lady claiming to have an appointment had asked directions to his office shortly after. The concierge hadn't seen her leave. But when he did his final rounds before locking up the building for the night, he found one of the windows in the ground-floor ladies' WC wide open.

# 2

# Gemini

Emily had had enough of today and decided to take a walk by the nearby canal to clear her head. Although she had been aware of her clairvoyant ability from an early age, she could only see into the past or future of another person, not her own. When Emily did experience her visions, they left her feeling physically exhausted.

As she turned and walked down some steps leading to the towpath, she shuddered and pulled her shawl closer around her shoulders. Looking up to the sky, she felt uneasy as she noticed the gathering cloud and felt a distinct chill in the air. A late October afternoon was rapidly turning into a dark, dismal night. As Emily walked along the narrow towpath, the fallen leaves crunched under her boots, and she could hear the trees rustling in the gathering breeze. A few minutes later, Emily heard footsteps behind her and began to quicken her pace. Looking ahead, she hoped to see other people walking in the opposite direction, but to her dismay,

there was no one. Even the houseboats she passed seemed unusually dark and unoccupied.

Then she heard her name being called. Emily glanced over her shoulder, thinking it might be her friend Lucy, who frequently walked her dog along the canal at this time of day. Seeing the figure of a young woman emerge from the mist, Emily froze on the spot, mesmerized. It was like staring at her own her reflection.

"Don't be scared," said the young woman. "I'm Alice, your twin sister. You knew you had a twin, didn't you?"

"Yes," whispered Emily. "How did you find me?"

"It wasn't hard," replied Alice, "but never mind that. I am here to be your sister, finally reunited. We should never have been parted at birth. Help me take revenge on those responsible."

Emily saw a glint of evil as she looked into her twin's eyes. A sense of fear and foreboding washed over her.

"No," replied Emily. "I don't want anything to do with revenge. I want to live my own life in my own way, without you or my adopted family. Please leave me alone. Go back to your own family and forget about me."

"You *are* my family," insisted Alice as she reached out and grabbed Emily's arm. "Look, I brought you a present, a sign of our solidarity." At that moment, Alice tried to place a Gemini charm bracelet into Emily's hand.

7

Emily pulled away, dropping the charm and breaking into a run. But the quicker she ran, the quicker she heard Alice's footsteps echo in hot pursuit. There seemed no escape along the narrow and dimly lit pathway. Suddenly, Emily slipped on a pile of wet leaves, banged her head on some broken railings, and fell into the ice-cold water of the canal.

Alice stood watching as Emily was dragged under by the weight of her saturated winter coat. Enraged by her rejection and consumed with jealousy, Alice then turned and continued walking. Her only thoughts now were how she was going to find out about Emily's upbringing and adopted family. Earlier that day, she had followed Emily to a psychiatrist's office. Well, thought Alice, getting Emily's file would be the perfect place to start.

# 3

# The Memento Box

October 30, 2009, late in the evening

After entering her apartment, Alice sat down on her sofa and lifted off her motorcycle helmet, then shook her head to release a cascade of long, dark hair. Reaching into the fake courier bag, she pulled out the stolen medical file. She then stood up and walked over to her desk, placing the file carefully in the desk drawer and turning the lock. Sitting back down, she reached into the bag again for the other treasure she had retrieved: a small box which contained photos and other keepsakes. Quickly sorting through it, she spied an envelope with "For Sophie" neatly written on the outside. Intrigued, she carefully opened the letter inside and began to read. There was an accompanying photo of a young couple embracing on a beach. Turning the photo over, she smiled as she read "Hastings, 1989." A plan of revenge began to form.

# 4

# Sophie

Sophie had always wanted to be a nurse and was so excited to be starting her final year of training at the Castle Hill Hospital in Whitechapel, London. It was the 5th of June, 1989. Today was Sophie's first day in theatre, and she had great hopes.

Carefully, Sophie checked her theatre cap, ensuring all her hair was neatly tucked in and her mask was properly in place. The theatre sister then arrived, and Sophie followed her in to watch an appendectomy. Halfway through, the sister asked Sophie to fetch an extra pack of swabs. "Just grab them and I will show you how to pass them to the scrub nurse using a sterile technique."

Sophie went through the double doors to the clean utility room, confident she knew where the swabs were after her initial orientation. Just as she was about to take them off the shelf, she heard a crash and what sounded like somebody falling. Sophie peeked around the corner from the shelves to see what looked like a young man in scrubs frantically getting to his feet and gathering up some surgical gloves that had fluttered to the floor.

"Oh, are you alright?" she asked.

The young man looked up and chuckled. "Yes, I seem to have found my size." He then extended his hand. "Charlie, medical student." Sophie reached out in response, their eyes met, and for a moment she seemed to forget herself. A second later, Sophie heard the doors to the theatre open, and Sister stood there, hands on hips.

"Nurse, is there a problem? I've already had to apologize to the surgeon. Now stop your chitter-chatter and follow me." She glared at Charlie. "If you need gloves, perhaps you might ask a nurse." She pointed at the pile of gloves on the floor. "Kindly clear those up. You're too late to scrub in for this case."

# 5

## "I Can't Cook"

A few days later, Sophie was walking with her friends Joanna and Helena. As they headed to the cafeteria on their last break of the shift, Sophie wondered what had happened to the medical student she had met, doubting she would ever see him again. The memory of his dark eyes and the touch of his hand made her smile.

As Sophie lined up to order her food, she felt a little tap on her shoulder. Turning around, she saw Charlie. This time, she noticed he was tall, with thick, brown hair which he swept back. "Sophie, isn't it?" he asked and smiled. "I just wanted to say hello after the other day."

Sophie could not believe her luck and tried to act calm, although her heart was racing.

"Are, are you in trouble, you know, with Sister?"

Charlie's smile turned into a wide grin as he adjusted his glasses. "Sister, always. But when I look at her like this," he said, making a sorrowful face, "she's a pussycat." Sophie began laughing at the thought.

A page came over the intercom, and Charlie excused himself to rush away. Sophie picked up her food, not realising she had left her paper napkins on the side.

As Sophie joined her two friends, she could already see their smiles and their eyes full of enquiry. Joanna looked up and then started stuffing her egg and chips, her cheeks filling like a little hamster. Helena, who was far too much of a lady for that, gave a discreet cough and sipped some water.

"I see you have a new friend," she whispered, leaning towards Sophie. "Is he going to join us?"

"Oh, you mean the medical student," Sophie replied, trying to sound nonchalant. "I bumped into him the other day, that's all."

"Oh, I know the one," chirped Joanna. "I overheard Sister saying he was a chocolate teapot." Helena tapped Joanna's foot as she saw the look on Sophie's face.

"He is not," replied Sophie crossly. "He's just new."

"Ok, keep your drawers on," Jo laughed. "He's headed over here right now." Sophie swung round to see Charlie walking towards them with a paper napkin, folded in half.

"Afternoon, ladies." Charlie looked at Sophie and placed the napkin strategically in her hand. "I think you forgot this," he said softly. "I wish I could join you, but I must go on rounds."

13

As Charlie hurried away, Sophie began to open the napkin but stopped as she saw a neatly written message: *Coffee? Sorry, I can't cook.* This was followed by a telephone number.

Sophie quickly placed the napkin into her uniform pocket and went back to her tea and scone.

That evening, Sophie returned to the nurses' home, exhausted from the week and the thought of her next assignment, which was due in just a few days. Opening the door to her little room, she set down her keys, hung up her coat, and lay down on the bed. As she was about to close her eyes, she became aware of the paper napkin crumpled in her pocket, forgotten. Reading the message again, she couldn't decide whether to call. It was just coffee, after all. So why not? She had just decided this when there was a knock at the door. It was Joanna.

"So?" said Jo.

"So what?" she replied.

"Are you going to the party? Thought you might like to get your glad rags on and boogie. Besides, you never know who might be there."

Sophie yawned in disinterest. "I'll think about it, Jo. But I want to have my supper now."

# 6

## Hug A Mug

Sophie closed the door, sat down on the bed, and stared at the note in her hand.

The compulsion to phone was irresistible. She had made up her mind that when the coast was clear, she would go down to the little phone booth on the ground floor and call.

Sophie unfolded the napkin and carefully dialled the number, then held her breath. After a few rings, there was an answer.

"Hello?"

Sophie recognised Charlie's voice.

After a nervous pause, she replied. "Hi, is that you, Charlie? It's Sophie. I, I read your message."

"Oh, hi Soph," he chuckled. "I wondered whether you'd like to go for coffee. There's a great little café by the dock. You know, a medical student's accommodation isn't that great and..."

"You can't cook," Sophie teased. "What's the café called?"

"Um, Hug A Mug."

"Yes, I know it, the one on the corner, overlooking the river."

"How about tomorrow?"

A Sunday fry-up sounded just the thing.

It wasn't often that Sophie had a weekend off, so when she did, it seemed special and exciting. On a Sunday, the markets were some of her favourite places in the East End, and she would stroll through, browsing the stalls for unique finds. Sophie adored the diversity and culture of the East End — immersing herself in sights such as colorful graffiti, listening to the sounds of numerous languages, and smelling the fragrances of different culinary dishes being prepared and offered for sale. However, when it came to Sunday breakfast, the Hug A Mug Café was a definite go-to, popular with students and locals alike.

Walking into Hug A Mug, Sophie was met by a wonderful aroma of egg and bacon and the sound of steam from a hot water container. Customers were bustling and chatting as they waited eagerly for their take-aways.

Sophie sat at a table near the window and picked up the brightly coloured menu. She felt hungry, so the traditional fry-up with baked beans seemed just the job.

"Can I take your order?" came a friendly voice. Sophie became aware of a portly middle-aged lady, hair tied back neatly in a bun and her Hug A Mug apron clean and bright.

"I haven't quite decided. I'm waiting for someone."

"Oh, aren't we all love?" she replied, laughing. "Cup of tea while you're deciding. We've got a Sunday special," and she placed a paper insert on the table.

"Thanks," replied Sophie.

A few minutes later, Sophie looked up to see Charlie entering the café. For a moment, she wasn't sure it was him. He was wearing some tight-fitting jeans, a Motörhead tee-shirt, a black leather jacket, and sunglasses.

Once he spotted her, he strode over and sat at the table, taking off his glasses and placing his jacket on the back of the chair.

"It is you then!" Sophie giggled.

"Ah yes, it's my disguise."

"Well, you don't look like a medical student I bumped into at the hospital."

"Thank God," Charlie replied, picking up the menu.

"Don't you want to be a doctor? asked Sophie.

"No," replied Charlie emphatically. "It's a family thing. My parents are doctors, and my grandmother won't hear of me doing anything else."

"Oh no. Well, what would you really like to do?"

Charlie considered for a moment. "Well, I love the countryside and animals. So farming would be my dream."

"Well, you never know what the future brings," said Sophie with hope.

Charlie beamed with amusement and took her hand as if to read her palm. The gesture seemed so natural.

"Oh, what do you see?" Sophie asked with excitement.

Charlie glanced up and then back down at her hand. "A journey," he replied. "I see you traveling. To a place you have always dreamed of visiting."

"That would be Paris. I was planning to go once I get through my finals."

At that moment, they were interrupted by the waitress.

"Two specials then, is it? Beans on the side. And a round of toast?"

"Rather," Charlie replied as he let go of Sophie's hand and leaned back on the seat. Sophie nodded her agreement, then poured them both tea and clutched her mug.

"So how long do you have left on your surgical rotation?"

"Just one more week, and then I have some personal study time."

"That sounds nice. Will you be coming back to Castle Hill?"

"I'm afraid not, but I'll still be in London while I'm preparing for exams," Charlie replied.

"Oh, well good luck with that. I'll be sorry to see you leave. Especially when we've only just met."

Charlie considered for a minute and took both of her hands in his. "I'd like to see you again. You can help me with revision, if you like. How about meeting at my place?"

There was no doubt, Sophie was in love, and she had to see him again.

"Orthopaedics it is, then," she jested. "Be prepared. I did well in my practicum."

# 7

## The First Time

Sophie sat on the number 15 bus, heading for Poplar Baths and armed with her orthopaedics books. Feeling full of excitement and anticipation, she reached into her handbag and carefully applied some fresh lipstick, then used a scrunchie to tie back her hair. She checked the piece of paper on which she had written Charlie's address. Just two more stops.

As Sophie stepped off the bus, she gazed in awe at the high-rise block. Not too bad for student accommodation. She looked again at her piece of paper and the directions Charlie had written down for her: TAKE THE LIFT TO THE 9TH FLOOR. MY FLAT IS 919.

Sophie pressed the button to summon the elevator but felt a little unnerved as she viewed the graffiti and smelled a stale stench when the door opened. *Oh well, at least it works,* she thought to herself. As she got out of the lift, she could see 919 just across the hall. Quickly, she adjusted her hair and took a deep breath, then pressed the buzzer and waited. A few seconds later, the door opened, and Charlie welcomed her with open arms. It was liked they had known each other forever, not just a few days. When he placed his arms around her and gently lifted her off the floor and into the apartment, her natural reaction was to place her arms around his shoulders, giggling. As Charlie set her down again, he drew her closer, and they instantly began to kiss.

Sophie felt in heaven. As the kiss finally finished, Charlie led her into the kitchen and opened the fridge door. "Glass of wine to help us study?" he asked.

"Love it," she answered.

As Sophie looked around the kitchen, she spotted a wok and some neatly prepared vegetables and chicken on a large wooden table.

"I thought you couldn't cook," she laughed.

"Well, sometimes I do," he answered. "Especially when I have such lovely company." Sophie sipped her wine and then, placing her glass on the table, reached for her bag and pulled out the textbooks. "I thought we could start with multiple choice," she said.

"Can't wait," Charlie answered as he poured himself some wine. "Make yourself comfortable on the couch. We can study before dinner."

Sophie snuggled next Charlie on the sofa and opened the book.

After an hour or so of satisfactory revision, Charlie started to cook the stir-fry, which smelt delicious. "This is a nice flat," Sophie commented.

"Not bad," Charlie replied. "My grandmother helps me out a lot. I share with one other guy. A dental student called Mark. He's hardly ever here though. Prefers his own company and studies in the library a lot."

After dinner, Sophie kicked off her shoes and snuggled back on the sofa next to Charlie. Closing her eyes, she whispered, "I am so comfortable; I could just forget the whole world."

Charlie gently stroked her hair and forehead, and whispered back, "Well, I'd love you to stay." Sophie sat up in surprise and turned towards him. "What, stay overnight? But I didn't bring anything with me."

Charlie smiled, looking thoughtful. "Well, I've got spare pyjamas, although they might be a bit big. Oh, and I'll introduce you to my friend Bones," he laughed.

"Bones," replied Sophie. "I thought his name was Mark."

Charlie took Sophie's hand and gently pulled her up from the sofa. "Follow me and I'll introduce you."

Charlie led Sophie into his bedroom, which appeared neat and tidy, with a bookshelf full of textbooks and below those, a stack of Motörhead albums.

Then she saw the skeleton in the corner. "Oh, this is Bones, I presume?"

"The one and only," he answered.

"And he stays in this room?" she asked.

"Well, most of the time." Charlie laughed. "Look, he's quite friendly," and he took hold of the skeleton's forearm, extending it as if to shake hands.

"Oh, how do you do?" Sophie said in her posh voice.

Charlie burst into laughter and rested back on the bed, patting the quilt by his side. Sophie looked a little hesitant and glanced at Bones. "I just feel like he's looking at us," she smiled.

"Oh, well he can go in the cupboard if you like," replied Charlie.

She laughed as he took Bones out of the room, returning with the bottle of wine and two fresh glasses. Charlie gently placed his arm around Sophie's waist, handing her another glass of wine. Their eyes met as they clinked glasses, and each took a sip of wine. Both Charlie and Sophie were overwhelmed with passion and desire for each other. Charlie set down his glass on the side, smiling, then gently placed Sophie's glass beside his. Leaning forward, he kissed her forehead, then pulling her closer, kissed her on the lips and then her neck. Sophie responded enthusiastically, running her hands through his hair and removing his glasses. What came next seemed only natural, as they began to make love and continued well into the night. Sophie had had relationships before, but not like this. This was so different.

In the early hours of the morning, there was the sound of the front door being opened, followed by footsteps and the noise of the kitchen light being switched on.

"What the fuck. Charlie, what the hell is Bones doing at the kitchen table? And why is he holding an empty glass next to the bottle of wine?"

Charlie scrambled to reach his dressing gown as Sophie clutched the duvet over her head, laughing.

"It's just Mark," he whispered. "He wasn't supposed to be back until later today." To Mark he replied, "Oh, he was a bit fed up and wanted a drink. You know how sensitive skeletons can be."

As Charlie opened the door, Mark looked at him with suspicion. "I see you've been studying then?" he said,

24

nodding at the textbooks. "Hungry, were you?" he asked, pointing to the plates and cutlery that had been washed up and placed in the drying rack.

"Look, I have a guest," Charlie explained, reaching for coffee cups.

"You old devil you," gasped Mark, patting Charlie on the back.

"Shush!!!" replied Charlie.

"Mum's the word," Mark answered, placing his finger to his lips. "Would your guest like coffee too?" he whispered.

"Her name is Sophie, and I'll ask her."

As Charlie carefully opened the bedroom door. Sophie was getting dressed. However, as she picked up her blouse, she noticed a wine stain on the front.

Charlie smiled, "Here, borrow one of my shirts," and he passed her one of his beloved Motörhead tees.

As Charlie made coffee and continued to chat to Mark, Sophie hurriedly finished dressing and tidied her hair. Shyly, she entered the kitchen and gladly took the mug of coffee that Charlie handed to her. He then introduced Sophie to Mark and Mark to Sophie. "You've already met Bones," he added, pointing to the skeleton still sitting in the chair.

"Well, lovely to meet you," said Mark, shaking Sophie's hand. "Charlie tells me you're a student nurse. What sort of nursing would you like to do?" he enquired.

"I'm not too sure yet," replied Sophie. "Cardiac perhaps, although I really like maternity. Perhaps I'll go into midwifery."

"Oh no," exclaimed Charlie. "I remember obstetrics well. The midwives were so bloody scary, I wanted to take the gas and air myself," he chuckled.

Sophie was suddenly aware of the time and the fact that she had to make it back for a late shift.

"I'll drive you," Charlie offered.

"No, that's fine," Sophie insisted. "The traffic is already building."

Charlie walked Sophie to the elevator and then kissed her on the cheek. "Thanks for last night," he whispered. "I'll call you later. After you get home from your late shift."

Sophie turned to him and blew a kiss as the elevator doors closed. *Oh my God*, she thought. *He introduced me to Mark as his girlfriend.*

# 8

## Should I Ask?

Sophie slipped through the double doors of the nursing accommodation and passed the office of the warden, who luckily was sorting mail and didn't seem to notice Sophie creep to the back staircase leading to the rooms. As Sophie approached her door, she noticed a note attached.

> *Called but you weren't in. See you on late.*
> *Jo and Helena*

Sophie collapsed on her bed and set the alarm. What a night it had been.

As the alarm rang, Sophie could not believe a whole four hours had passed. She headed for a shower. Just one more late shift to get through, and her theatre rotation would be complete.

When Sophie entered the staff room for hand-over, she couldn't help noticing the silence. Sister looked at her directly. "Thank you for joining us, nurse. You can team with the circulating nurse. That's Nurse Anderson," she continued, smiling at Joanna. "You can scrub in with Nurse Lewis." Jo had taken to theatre nursing like a duck to water, and Sister had her in mind as a new staff nurse in her department.

As everyone got up to attend to their duties, Jo whispered, "What happened to you? Or shouldn't I ask?"

"No, you shouldn't, but I'll tell you later anyway," replied Sophie, blushing.

Shortly after she had returned to her room at shift's end, there was a knock at her door, and a voice said, "Phone call for Sophie." She opened the door and ran down the stairs to the little phone booth, where the receiver had been carefully balanced on the ledge.

"Hello," Sophie chirped.

"Hi Sophie, it's me," Charlie answered.

"Hi," said Sophie, excited to speak but trying not to yawn.

"How did your shift go? I've been thinking about you and last night all day."

"It was fine, apart from Sister glaring at me. Mind you, she glares at everyone."

"Oh dear," replied Charlie. "Well look. I can't wait to see you again. I'm heading for the coast next weekend. My annual trip of thanksgiving to my grandmother. Grandma is very sweet. She has a massive house in Hastings. Welcomes my friends. I'm guessing you have some time off between finishing your practicum and starting your next theory block. Want about a trip to the coast?"

"That, that sounds wonderful," answered Sophie with excitement.

"Hastings it is, then," he replied.

# 9

# Grandma

Charlie drew up outside the Nurse Home, sounding the car horn to let Sophie know he had arrived. His faithful little Austin Mini Metro was raring to go. Sophie ran out and jumped into front seat next to Charlie, throwing her bag on the back seat.

"Good to see you," Charlie kissed her on the cheek and gently placed a hand on her knee.

Sophie noticed the usual curtain twitchers at the windows, looking out onto the street. "Better go before we're photographed," joked Sophie.

Charlie smiled and drove off, heading for the motorway.

A few minutes later, he began to brief her about the trip.

"Look, just to let you know, my grandmother is quite attentive. I'm her only grandson, and seeing me graduate means everything to her. The family tradition. When my parents moved out to South Africa due to my father's job, she was absolutely devasted and determined she would bring me back and put me through medical school."

"Well, I am sure she is very nice," replied Sophie. "Um, how will she feel about you having a girlfriend though?"

"I've told her about you," answered Charlie. "She didn't say much but said she was looking forward to meeting you."

As Charlie drew up outside their destination, Sophie began to feel a little in awe as she gazed at a large house surrounded by meticulously manicured gardens. "I thought she lived alone," whispered Sophie. Glancing towards the front windows, she had noticed two ladies looking out, one elderly and elegantly dressed, presumably Grandma, and what looked like a middle-aged woman, nicely dressed and with her hair meticulously styled into a bun.

"She has a housekeeper, Mrs. Jackson, although I call her the gate keeper," Charlie replied. "Acts on my grandmother's orders and knows everything."

Charlie grasped Sophie's hand, sensing that she was nervous. "Look, it will be fine, she won't eat you. Well, not the first time she meets you, anyway," he joked.

Mrs. Jackson opened the door and ushered Charlie and Sophie in. "Grandma!" Charlie called.

"Charlie, come into the living room, and bring your friend; I want to meet her. Mrs. Jackson will bring us tea," came a strong voice.

Charlie opened the door to the living room, and his grandmother turned around to greet them. Charlie gave her a gentle hug and then began to introduce her to Sophie.

"Hello," said Sophie softly, reaching out to shake her hand. Charlie's grandmother smiled and shook her hand in response. However, Sophie couldn't help feeling she was being looked at in a judgemental way.

"Sophie is a student nurse," Charlie stated enthusiastically.

"Yes, so you told me."

"I'm thinking of going into midwifery once I've had some staff nurse experience," Sophie added.

"Really, how sweet," replied Grandma in a disinterested manner, turning her attention to Charlie. "Well, let's all have some tea."

Mrs. Jackson entered the room and set down a tray of tea and a decorative plate of biscuits. "Oh, wonderful," announced Sophie. "Shall I be mother?"

There was a sudden silence, and Mrs. Jackson stared directly at Charlie's grandmother. "Oh no, dear, we wouldn't want Mrs. Jackson to feel like she is not doing her job."

Mrs. Jackson poured the tea and handed the cups in pecking order. First, she carefully handed a particular China cup to Charlie's grandmother, and then one to Charlie. Sophie was handed her tea last and noticed that Mrs. Jackson would not even make eye contact. "Thank you," said Sophie politely, not daring to take a biscuit until she was invited.

"Mrs. Jackson has prepared a guest room for you. Why don't you unpack, and then I want to tell you all about the plans for my birthday party. Once you are both settled in, come back down, and we can all discuss the arrangements."

As Sophie came down the stairs, she could hear Charlie and his grandmother talking.

"Your parents have made their usual excuses, as expected. At least I won't have to worry about trying to be nice to them," exclaimed Grandma.

"Grandma, I am sure they would have made it if they could. You know how involved they are in their work," replied Charlie in defence.

"Poppycock," cried his grandmother in response. "Since I disinherited them, they don't want to know me. However, I invited a friend of yours to come over. In fact, she's coming to London on an assignment with the marketing firm she works for and has also volunteered to help Mrs. Jackson with my party arrangements. I think you'll be as excited as I am." Charlie looked at his grandmother, wondering who she might mean.

"It's Delores!" she exclaimed. Charlie pictured the neighbours' twelve-year-old daughter he had befriended many years ago. They would play in the garden treehouse and imitate animals. "And Charlie, I am counting on you to make her feel welcome. Do you understand me?"

"Yes, Grandma, but I haven't seen her for years."

"Exactly," she replied. "And a fine young woman she has turned into. Delores comes from a good family, who ensured she received an excellent education."

Charlie's heart sank. Oh God, was this Grandma's matchmaking?

"She is arriving on Monday, in readiness for my party next week. I will expect you to be here when she arrives. Your friend is welcome but will have to stay elsewhere," Grandma continued.

Sophie made a discreet entrance, trying to pretend she had not heard the conversation.

"Why don't you show Sophie the beach. I am sure you two would like some sea air before dinner."

As they walked hand in hand along the beach, looking out to sea, Charlie turned to Sophie. "Look, when Grandma has had her party and we've finished our exams, let's go away. Paris, if you like. Just you and me. Celebrating."

Celebrating, thought Sophie. "I would love that so much," she responded with excitement, picturing them sharing a glass of champagne in her much longed for destination.

"Good. Let's get a picture of us on the beach," he suggested, producing a new Polaroid camera.

As an elderly gentleman walking his dog approached, Charlie asked politely whether he would mind taking a photo. Obliging, he waited while Charlie and Sophie had perched on a large log and were hugging one another. A perfect picture.

The following day, Sophie and Charlie climbed back into their car, leaving the quaint seaside town of Hastings. The sun was beginning to set, casting a warm glow over the landscape as they drove along the motorway towards Poplar. A little while into the journey, Sophie's mind drifted back to her encounter with Mrs. Jackson. Sophie was curious to know more about her. Sophie hadn't met many housekeepers and was intrigued. Mrs. Jackson wasn't old, but her clothing and mannerisms seemed from a time gone by. When Sophie had managed to make eye contact with her, she had sensed a deep sadness and felt there was more to this woman's story.

"What's Mrs. Jackson's first name?" Sophie asked.

"I don't know," answered Charlie. "Everyone just calls her Mrs. Jackson. She's been Grandma's assistant and carer for the past two years now. Grandma had numerous housekeepers before her, but none of them seemed to stay long. When Mrs. Jackson turned up, they just seemed to hit it off. To the agency's relief," laughed Charlie. "Why? What's the fascination?"

"Oh, nothing," replied Sophie. "I just think, well, she didn't like me."

"Don't take it personally," Charlie responded. "She's like that with everyone and is extremely protective over Grandma."

"What about Mr. Jackson?"

"Oh, no one knows," Charlie answered, then said jokingly, "Perhaps he's dead, perhaps Mrs. Jackson murdered him, his body never to be found. I mean, she does cook some unusual recipes."

"Does she?" Sophie gasped. "What's in them?" she giggled.

'Well that's the thing," Charlie whispered. "She won't tell anyone."

"And what do you think she will make of Delores?"

"Delores?" answered Charlie, feeling cold at the thought of having to entertain her on his grandmother's orders. "I'm not sure," he answered. "From what I remember, she was a tall, gorky tomboy with braces. Anyway, let's not talk about her or Mrs. Jackson. Look, are you hungry? Let's go for an Indian," continued Charlie, desperately wanting to change the subject.

Feeling reassured, Sophie said, "I'd love to."

"That's settled then," Charlie smiled. "Hey, do you mind if I put on some music?"

"Ooh, let me guess," teased Sophie. "Motörhead, by any chance?"

Charlie laughed as he reached for a cassette from his beloved collection. "Come on, you know you love singing to this one."

"Why not?" she exclaimed.

As the music began, Charlie wound down his window, allowing a cool breeze to enter the car, and turned up the volume. Then both of them began to sing along to "Ace of Spades."

> *If you like to gamble*
> *I tell you, I'm your man*
> *You win some, lose some.*

As they arrived back in the familiar surroundings of the East End, Charlie remembered he needed to pick up the plane tickets to Paris, which he had secretly booked over the phone.

"Oh no, I forgot to post something for Grandma! Now I'm in trouble. Do you mind if I pull in for second? There's a post office just around the corner. We'll go straight to the restaurant after."

"Not at all," replied Sophie, who was just glad to be back home. Once around the corner and out of sight, Charlie hurriedly entered the travel agent's and picked up the tickets, slipping them into the inner pocket of his leather jacket.

Charlie and Sophie entered the Indian Oasis and were instantly enveloped by a wonderful aroma of spices and the sound of traditional Indian music. As they were seated at a table for two, the waiter lit the candle. Sophie thought it looked very romantic. In no time at all, they were pouring white wine and tucking into a selection of their favourite dishes.

"This is wonderful," Sophie commented.

Charlie smiled as he placed his napkin on the table and reached into his jacket pocket. "I have a surprise for you." He pulled out a wallet with a travel agency logo and passed it to her. Excitedly, Sophie gently opened it up and saw the plane tickets and then the destination: Paris.

"Oh my God, I don't know what to say."

"You don't have to say anything, just be packed and ready to go two weeks today."

"But this is so close to your grandmother's birthday celebrations."

"Yes, I know," replied Charlie. "Believe me, we will both need to get away."

Sophie reached for her wine. "Well, here's to Paris," she stated, raising her glass. "Ooh là là," she added as the glasses clinked.

Charlie leaned froward. "I do hope so," he whispered and kissed her gently on the lips.

# 10

## Delores

As the plane came to a halt at the gate and the seatbelt sign pinged, Delores stood up. Being tall and slender, she easily retrieved her bag from the overhead bin. Not having been back to the UK since she was a child, she was full of excitement. The invitation to the grand birthday celebrations was a wonderful excuse to take off and head for an adventure. A letter accompanying the invitation had mentioned that Charlie would meet her at the train station and drive her to the cottage.

Her mind went back to a wonderful summer when they had played games and raced around the garden, pretending to be animals. Delores always wanted to be a fox, clever and cunning, whereas Charlie loved badgers. With bag in hand and stepping onto the airport's moving walkway, she felt like a woman on a mission. And she was. Charlie's grandmother was worth a fortune in land and property. A family rift with Charlie's parents had led her to make Charlie, her only grandson, sole heir to her estate. Delores was determined to find out all about him and his present situation.

Charlie drew up in front of the train station, wondering whether he would even recognise Delores. He just wanted to get this over with and be able to return to Sophie. As he slowed down at the pickup point, he spotted a tall, elegant lady dressed in a smart trouser suit, with an expensive set of luggage. He wound down his window. "Delores," he called.

Delores waved and hastened over to the car. "Charlie," she cried. Being a gentleman, Charlie got out and placed her luggage in the boot, then opened the passenger door.

As they began the drive, Delores dove into conversation. "I am so happy to see you again after all these years. We have so much catching up to do. Your grandmother's party sounds fabulous, like she's really pushing the boat out."

"Yes," Charlie smiled. "I think this has been in the planning for some time."

"And how's life with you?" Delores enquired. "Med school going well?"

"Ok," Charlie replied. "You know."

"And…" But before Delores could finish her next sentence, she spotted his photo key ring, with the picture of Charlie and Sophie.

"Is that your girlfriend?"

"Yes," Charlie replied. "Her name is Sophie. She'll be at the party. I'll introduce you."

"That's wonderful, I would love that," Delores replied, eager to meet and eliminate any competition as soon as she could.

As they pulled up outside the cottage, Mrs. Jackson opened the door but somehow seemed different. "Come in, dear, don't get cold. Welcome to the cottage." It was like she knew Delores, but as far as he was aware, they had never met before.

Delores entered the living room and embraced Charlie's grandmother. "Thank you for inviting me. I am really looking forward to your birthday party and helping in any way I can."

"It's a pleasure to see you. How was your trip? And you must tell me all about your new job," Charlie's grandmother replied. "Charlie, why don't you see if Mrs. Jackson has finished making tea. Delores, make yourself comfortable on the sofa."

As Charlie left the room, Delores couldn't wait to find out more about Sophie. "Charlie tells me he has a girlfriend," began Delores.

Charlie's grandmother considered for a minute. Then, like a schoolgirl telling a secret within earshot, "Well," she whispered, "a sweet girl, a student nurse, but, you know, a passing fad, I fancy. He'll know when the right woman comes along. Someone suitable for his class and profession."

"Oh, I'm sure," Delores replied with enthusiasm. "It's not serious, then?"

"Not as far as I'm concerned," answered Grandma. Aware that Charlie was coming down the stairs, she winked at Delores and poured another cup of tea.

"Why don't you sit next to Delores?" his grandmother urged. Wordlessly, he sat next to her, realising as he did that she smiled and edged closer towards him.

"Now Delores, you're in charge of flowers and seating, and Mrs. Jackson will oversee catering. There will be a pianist. And a cake, of course. As you know, I have chosen to hold the party at the Crown Hotel."

"Sounds wonderful," murmured Charlie. "The thing is, Grandma, I'm leaving for Paris the following morning. Both Sophie and I will be finished exams and, well, we need a break."

There was an uncomfortable silence, and Charlie's grandmother set down her teacup with a frown. "I see. We'll discuss this later, dear. For now, I want a picture of you and Delores, long-lost friends, reunited after years," she announced.

"Oh, do you mind?" pleaded Delores, looking into his eyes. "It would be such a lovely memory to put in your grandmother's party scrapbook."

"Suppose not," replied Charlie reluctantly.

Charlie's grandmother clapped her hands with glee. "Mrs. Jackson, bring the Polaroid, would you?" she called.

Mrs. Jackson quickly appeared with the new instamatic camera, beaming from ear to ear.

"For goodness' sake, Charlie, smile and put your arm around Delores," directed Grandma. Charlie obediently placed his arm around Delores's shoulders and smiled. Delores intentionally snuggled into Charlie and beamed as Mrs. Jackson took the picture.

"Wonderful. One more, in case the first one doesn't develop. One, two, three," she counted. Delores suddenly turned towards Charlie and gave him a quick peck on the cheek. Before he could move, the camera clicked.

Charlie pulled away from Delores, took a breath, and turned to his grandmother, "Well, I hope you will excuse me, but I need to pack and get ready to drive back to London."

"Yes, it gets dark early, and the weather forecast is not that good. Could you meet me in the dining room before you leave? I wish to discuss your trip."

Delores stood and gathered up the tea tray. "I'll take these through to Mrs. Jackson," she said, feeling she should make an exit.

As Charlie reached the bottom of the stairs and placed his weekend bag in the hallway, he was aware that the door to the dining room was partially open. The lamplight shone through into the hallway.

He knocked on the door. "Grandma," he called.

"Come in, dear, and take a seat a minute. Now," she barked, "your trip to Paris. What is the meaning of it?"

"Well," replied Charlie, "I love Sophie, and I want to take her away from the stress of exams and working in a hospital."

"Nonsense," cried his grandmother. "Having a friend while you're studying is one thing, but you're about to graduate from medical school and become the next doctor in the family. I might not have many years left, but I'll be damned if I'll stand by and see you throw all that education away like a love-struck puppy. I saw your father marry for what he described as love, and I promptly disinherited him. Charlie, I don't want you to make a big mistake. I want to see you marry a suitable, well brought-up young lady, and to see my first great-grandchild born before I die. I am not saying Sophie is not a nice girl, and I am sure she will make someone a nice wife. But not you."

Charlie tried to conceal his anger at his grandmother's words and her attempt at matchmaking.

"Grandma," he replied firmly, "I am going to take Sophie to Paris, and as far as I am concerned, she is a suitable girl. I am in love with her."

"Charming," replied Grandma acidly. "Take her to Paris, and make it a fond farewell."

"I will be taking Sophie to Paris, but it will not be to say farewell," replied Charlie.

"Then you are a fool, and I hope she is worth forfeiting the millions you stand to inherit," replied Grandma, throwing her hands into the air and shaking her head.

Shocked, Charlie knew that she meant it.

"Look, I need to say goodbye, Grandma," Charlie replied softly. "I'll see you next weekend at your party."

"Yes, whatever dear," she answered, turning away to look out of the window.

He picked up his bag and headed to the car. As he sat behind the wheel, he was determined not to be intimidated by his grandmother's words or wishes. However, if it was a great-grandchild she was longing for, then maybe he had a plan. Sophie adored babies and wanted to be a midwife. He wanted her to be his wife. Paris wasn't going to be a fond farewell, not if he had anything to with it. It was a city of romance and love. The perfect setting to make a baby.

# 11

# The Birthday Party

Dolores looked stunning in her sleek, full-length, backless evening gown. Her short, dark hair, styled in a bob, lay neatly on her shoulders, and a sparkling headband and matching necklace completed the outfit. Attentively, she placed the name cards at the table, ensured each table had clean table-cloths and matching napkins, and carefully arranged a small vase of flowers. Mrs. Jackson then appeared and seemed very pleased as she walked around, inspecting Delores's work. She then handed her a pile of decorative menus and asked Delores to place them beside the name cards.

"A few people with allergies," she informed her. "I don't think we have anything on the menu that will be a problem." Delores looked at the list and spotted Sophie's name. Beside was an allergy alert: lavender. Delores gave a wicked smile. How awful, lavender was so lovely. She remembered the aromatherapy course she had taken and her favourite perfumed body lotion, which she now intended to use.

Charlie and Sophie arrived together, handing presents to Mrs. Jackson and making their way into the ballroom. Everything looked exquisite, and the mellow mood was set by a pianist and the gentle voice of a singer performing "As Time Goes By." Guests were greeted with a glass of champagne and shown to their tables. Sophie was in awe as she looked around at the magnificent surroundings and the lavish menu. Charlie pulled out her chair and assisted her like a gentleman. He looked handsome in his smart suit, crisp white shirt, and bow tie. Sophie was careful not to crease her brand-new dress, a beautiful emerald-green chiffon worn off the shoulder.

"You look gorgeous," Charlie whispered as Sophie placed herself in the chair.

After a sumptuous dinner, Charlie made a speech extolling his grandmother and thanking everyone who had attended and made the party possible. Sophie was sitting alone at the table, and Delores saw her chance. She grabbed a carefully contrived bouquet of flowers that had lavender discreetly hidden among the other flowers, then strolled over to the reception desk and informed the receptionist that they had just arrived for one of the guests.

As Sophie sipped her wine, a waiter approached her, stating that some flowers had been left for her in reception. Thinking these were a present from Charlie, Sophie went to reception and took up the beautiful bouquet, admiring them and naturally wanting to bury her nose in the fragrant aroma. Immediately, she sensed the lavender and began to cough as she felt her lips tingling and cheeks flushing. Sophie felt suddenly panicked as she remembered she had left her EpiPen in her other bag at home.

Delores, who'd been watching carefully, rushed over. "Oh my god, Sophie, are you ok?" Quickly, she summoned the porter. "Drive Sophie to the A&E." Earlier, she had ascertained from Mrs. Jackson that the hospital was only a five-minute drive away. "Now don't you worry, Sophie. I'll let Charlie know what is happening and tell him to join you."

Charlie returned to the table and started to look around for Sophie, feeling a little panicked at not seeing her. Delores approached him. "Are you looking for Sophie?"

"Yes, I am," he answered. "Have you seen her?"

"Oh, well I saw her dash off in a car with the porter. She seemed in a hurry and said to tell you she'd be back soon. Why don't you go and get changed out of your formal wear? I'm sure she'll be back soon. Look, I'll show you to your room."

Delores grabbed the key to the hotel room and led Charlie up the winding stairs. As he opened the door, Delores followed him in and went over to the dressing table, where a tray with coffee and tea were kept above the minibar. "Fancy a drink while you're waiting? Why don't you take your shoes off and loosen your tie. I'll pour you one."

Feeling hazy with the amount of champagne he had already imbibed, Charlie did as she suggested. Delores investigated the minibar and reached for the champagne, then poured them both a glass. "To Grandma," she toasted and giggled. Charlie echoed her words.

"Look, why don't I go down and watch for Sophie coming back? I'll show her where you are."

Delores went to reception and saw the porter returning through the door.

"How is Sophie?"

"Well, not too bad. Treated for an allergic reaction. Out of it, though, so they're keeping her for the rest of the night. They told her she should keep her EpiPen with her all the time."

"Oh, poor girl. I hope she's better soon," Delores said disingenuously, then abruptly returned to Charlie's room.

Gently opening the door, she saw the light from the bathroom shining onto the bed. The champagne had gotten the better of him, and he had decided to wait for Sophie in bed. Delores stood still for a moment. Seeing Charlie's naked chest, her feelings of attraction were overwhelming. Sophie wasn't going to have him, she was. Delores glided over and switched off the light, plunging the room into darkness.

Thinking it was Sophie returning, he pulled back the sheets and patted the mattress. "At last, I've been waiting for you. Get in here. Come to bed."

49

Delores slipped in silently beside him. As she lay there, Charlie rolled over and drew her close. Elated and with no desire to resist, Delores began to kiss him passionately.

As daylight streamed in through the window, Charlie opened his eyes and reached over to the bedside cabinet for his glasses. Glancing at the clock, he saw it was only 5 a.m. He could hear the shower and decided to call out.

"Hey Soph, what happened last night? Are you ok? We need to say goodbye to Grandma and get going back to London. Our flight leaves this evening. Do you want coffee?"

As Charlie got up to make coffee, he heard the shower switch off and the door of the bathroom open.

"Is that for me? Wonderful. Cream and sugar, please."

Charlie froze, not wanting to turn around but recognising Delores's voice.

He put down the coffee mugs and faced her. Delores stood wearing a hotel dressing gown, with a towel wrapped around her head in a turban.

"What the hell are you doing here, and where the hell is Sophie?" Charlie growled.

Delores sat at the end of the bed and leaned forward. "I stayed at your invitation, and it was amazing."

"Delores, I did not invite you into my bed. Now where the hell is Sophie. I want to know, *now*."

Delores rolled her eyes. "She went to hospital, but she's ok."

"Which hospital? Why the fuck didn't you tell me?"

"I just did," replied Delores. "Anyway, you were drunk."

Charlie grabbed a pile of her clothes and threw them towards her. "Get dressed and get out of here." He hurriedly began to dress.

After pulling her clothes on, Delores headed for the door.

"Do you want me to call the hospital? She's probably on her way back."

"No, I told you, just go."

"Ok, well, cheerio. Umm, have a nice trip to Paris." As she opened the door, she turned and blew a kiss.

Charlie grabbed his jacket and keys. He would go straight to the hospital, collect Sophie, and get them the hell out of there.

As he arrived in the reception area, he spotted a taxi drawing up to the doors and what looked like Sophie in the back seat.

He raced out and opened the door. "Soph, are you ok? What happened? The last time I looked, you were at the table."

"I tried calling your room," said Sophie, "but the receptionist said no one was answering. Did Delores tell you what happened?"

"All she said was that you went off in a hurry and were going to be back soon."

Sophie looked at him in disbelief. "Did she tell you that I had an allergic reaction to the flowers you sent me?"

"Flowers?" replied Charlie. "I didn't send you flowers."

"Then who did?" Sophie answered. "Who would do such a thing?"

Charlie tried to conceal his anger as it all fitted together. Delores!

"Look, let's check out and get back to London. Do you think you'll be ready for Paris?"

"Try stopping me!" stated Sophie as she reached out and gave him a hug.

Charlie took her hand in a protective way. "Well, let's get the suitcases."

"Shouldn't we say goodbye?"

"I already have," he replied grimly.

# 12

## Paris

As the taxi drew up in front of the little hotel, Sophie was mesmerized by its beauty and the array of roses and other flowers that surrounded the doorway.

"It's gorgeous," she gasped.

"Yes, not bad," Charlie smiled.

As they entered the hotel, Sophie took in the exquisite décor and French ambience. Looking up, she saw an elegant chandelier. Below her feet was an artistically tiled floor.

After they had checked in, the porter showed them to a quaint elevator and pressed the call button. "Oh, very Agatha Christie," whispered Sophie.

"Well, Miss Marple, we'll keep a lookout for anything suspicious," joked Charlie as the elevator moved upwards and then came sharply to a halt at the fourth floor.

As the porter opened their door and placed their bags on the floor, Sophie couldn't believe how wonderful the room was. She ran to the French doors that led out onto a balcony. "Oh, look at the view, it's wonderful! I can't wait to explore."

"Well, let's unpack and go and get dinner. Mark has stayed here and recommended a little bistro nearby."

As they stepped out of the hotel, Charlie thought how stunning Sophie looked in her navy and white polka dot dress, with the late afternoon sunshine glistening in her red hair.

When they reached the end of the road, a bistro came into sight. The air was warm enough for them to sit outside at a charming little table. Sophie picked up the menu and started to read, feeling her schoolgirl French would finally come in handy. She loved the bistro's enchanting atmosphere. Soft lighting and the sound of jazz music playing overhead seemed so romantic.

The waiters were all smartly dressed in black trousers, crisp white shirts, black ties, and matching server aprons.

"It's not like Poplar, is it?" she giggled.

"Thank God," replied Charlie.

Carte

Soupe
L'oignon français
Bouillabaisse

Entrées
Coq au vin
Bœuf bourguignon
Steak frites
Quiche lorraine
Saumon en papillote

Dessert
Tarte frangipane aux poires
Gâteau trois chocolats

As they finished the meal, Charlie looked up and suggested they take an evening walk. He had mapped out a route to the Pont des Arts. He couldn't think of a more romantic place to go and talk to Sophie about his plan. As they approached a spot about halfway across the bridge, they embraced and looked out. The Eiffel Tower sparkled magically in the distance.

"Oh, this is just the best," sighed Sophie and reached for her Polaroid. "I'll always remember this." Once she had taken the picture, Charlie placed his arm around her waist and wondered whether this might be the right moment to speak to her about his idea of starting a family. He hoped so much that she would want to have a baby.

"I'm really glad you're loving our trip here," began Charlie. "It's so special to be here with you, and I want this to be a time we will both hold in our hearts."

"Absolutely," Sophie replied. "We must take something back with us — a painting, a special souvenir. Do you have anything in mind?" she asked curiously.

"I do," Charlie smiled. "I tell you what. Why don't we make our way back to the hotel, and we'll discuss things over a glass of wine." Feeling a sudden chill and change in temperature, she linked her arm through Charlie's and snuggled into him.

As the evening drew in and darkness fell, they walked through quaint, narrow streets with traditional lampposts

and tall buildings either side. Finally, they found a cab to take them back to the hotel. Sophie looked out of the cab window at the gathering clouds.

"Oh no, it's going to rain, and I didn't bring a jacket."

"You can wear mine," Charlie said as he took off his jacket and protectively wrapped it around her shoulders.

As they drew up outside the hotel and began the short walk to the entrance, there was an enormous clap of thunder and a sudden downpour of torrential rain. "Let's make a run for it!" said Sophie, trying to cover both of them as they ran towards the hotel. They splashed into a large puddle, the water drenching them both. "Look there's another one," Sophie said in exasperation, pointing to another large puddle that had formed just outside the hotel entrance.

"Well, I'll carry you over this one," he said.

"Oh Mr. Darcy," joked Sophie as Charlie swept her off her feet and carried her into the hotel lobby. They dashed for the elevator, dripping all over the floor.

As they entered their room, Sophie began to shiver. "I need to get out of these clothes and into the shower."

"Couldn't agree more," replied Charlie, "let's go," playfully tugging at her clothes.

As they entered the powerful shower, the warm water rained down and the steam began to rise in the cubical. Sophie placed her arms around Charlie's shoulders as they drew each other closer and began a long, lingering kiss.

Much later, as they stepped out of the shower, Charlie turned to Sophie. "There's something I wanted to ask you. I know you like babies. Do you want children of your own one day?"

Sophie felt a little surprised and leaned back on the pillow, sipping a glass of wine. "Yes, of course, one day. Why? When were you thinking of?"

"Well, there's no time like the present," he joked as pulled her closer and loosened her bathrobe.

"Charlie, are you serious?"

"Never been more," he replied.

As they lay back on the bed, there was a knock on the door. "Salut, c'est le service d'étage!"

"Juste une minute!" Charlie called out. "I forgot I had ordered champagne for us."

"Fabulous." Sophie grabbed her robe and opened the door. A maid entered, pushing a tray; she seemed used to unintentionally interrupting moments of passion. Quickly placing the tray on the table, she smiled and said, "Bonne nuit."

The following morning, Charlie and Sophie set out on a day of sightseeing, exploring the city from the Eiffel Tower to the Arc de Triomphe and then Notre Dame. Walking along the banks of the River Seine, they paused for a moment to watch an entertainer miming.

As they headed towards the hotel, Sophie noticed a small tattoo shop and pulled Charlie towards the window. "I've always wanted a tattoo. Look at that one." Sophie pointed to a picture of a heart and, in the centre, the Eiffel Tower. In a semicircle above the heart was *Vous souvenez-vous de Paris?* Do you remember Paris? A matching semicircle below said *Comment pourrais-j'oublier.* How could I forget. "It's beautiful," she whispered.

"Well, if you're sure," Charlie said. "I've got a Motörhead one, as you know."

"Yes," she replied, squeezing his hand.

"I need to get a few things for our return. Why don't I meet you back here in a couple of hours?"

Sophie entered the tattoo parlour, which seemed enchanting. Between her schoolgirl French and the artist's English, Sophie was able to get the tattoo she wanted.

The weekend had gone so fast, and Charlie dreaded returning to London from what had been a wonderful and memorable trip. He knew he would have to face his grandmother. He would simply say they'd had a wonderful time, and he would now be looking for his first job. He decided to tell her that Sophie was concentrating on getting into midwifery school and they remained friends. Hopefully that would stall her disapproval until he could announce other news.

# 13

## Not This Time

It was a cold and rainy day in Poplar, but Sophie didn't care as she disappeared into the bathroom with her box containing the pregnancy testing kit. She was surprised that it could have happened so soon after stopping the contraceptive pill. Excited and nervous, she waited the two minutes with her eyes closed, praying for a positive result.

As she looked down and saw the single line meaning negative, she couldn't believe it. Maybe it was wrong, a faulty kit. She'd had no period for eight weeks now, and she could have sworn she had some of the early pregnancy signs.

Her eyes swelled with tears as she opened the bathroom door and made her way into the kitchen, where Charlie was making them breakfast. Not seeing her face, he called out, "So, am I cooking for three?"

There was an eerie silence, and Charlie turned and saw her sobbing, still holding the test in her hand.

"It must be wrong; I was sure it was going to be positive."

"Look, you know it takes time. Let's make an appointment to see your GP. Have a few routine tests. I'm sure there is nothing of concern. It's just not positive this time."

Charlie hugged her, trying not show his disappointment, then took her hand and said, "Now, what about this breakfast?"

After they had eaten, Sophie composed herself and dialled the number of her GP's office to make an appointment.

# 14

## The Booking

Delores reached the grand door of the private gynaecologist's office, reassured she was in the right place as she read the shining brass plaque: Dr. Leila Patel.. She had performed a home pregnancy test but wanted definite confirmation of her suspicions. Excitedly, she sat down, sipping percolated coffee provided by the smiling and smartly dressed receptionist. Delores gazed around the room, admiring the colourful pictures and artwork that decorated the waiting area. One wall was decorated with pictures of Dr. Patel holding newborns, and thank you cards from grateful patients.

As she was called in, Delores took a deep breath and clutched her new designer handbag, a birthday gift from an admirer.

"Hello, take a seat, Miss Brown. I have the blood results, and I can tell you that the home test was correct. You are most definitely pregnant."

Delores squeezed her purse and beamed, her heart racing with joy as she tried to take in the news.

"Now, can I take it this is a wanted pregnancy? You and your partner are happy?"

"My partner, um, yes. He will be over the moon," replied Delores.

"Well congratulations. Let's do an initial exam and booking. Where do you plan to have the baby?"

"I haven't really thought about it. Perhaps at St. Thomas's," Delores replied.

"Good choice. I deliver there. I think you will like the Westminster Suite; it has the most wonderful views."

As Delores left the office, she felt elated. Now to break the news to Charlie. She had his number somewhere and would call him that evening.

# 15

## It's Your Baby

Charlie was sitting in a comfortable chair, listening to music and reading the newspaper, when the phone rang. Thinking it would be Sophie after her interview for staff nurse on general medicine, he jumped up to answer.

"Hey," answered Charlie, "how did it go?"

There was a pause, and then Delores began to talk. "Hi, Charlie, it's Delores. I'm calling because, well, because we need to talk."

"Oh," he replied in surprise. "Is it Grandma? Is everything ok?"

Delores hesitated. "No, she's fine. It's about us."

Charlie gave a deep sigh. "Look, Delores, I don't know how I can make it any clearer. There is no us, and there never will be."

"Well, there is now," exclaimed Delores. "I'm pregnant. I've just been to see my doctor to confirm it."

"Congratulations," said Charlie. "So shouldn't you be discussing this with the father?"

"I am," she replied.

"Don't be ridiculous, Delores, we've never even—," Charlie stopped mid-sentence as he remembered his grandmother's party.

"You're not bloody serious. This is a joke, right?"

"No, it's not a joke, Charlie, it's for real, and I'm keeping the baby."

Charlie was lost for words. He felt his brow and palms become sweaty and his breathing increase.

"What do you want?" he asked.

"I want to talk to you in person, and no, I have no plans to return to South Africa. In fact, I've been offered a job here in London, and it will fit in with being a mother. Let's meet up at the weekend, shall we?"

"Ok, but not here."

"Why don't you come down to Hastings? That way, we can drop in and break the news to Grandma."

Charlie remained silent. This was nothing but a nightmare, and his mind was alive with thoughts of what he was going to do. God, what about Sophie?

"Are you still there?" asked Delores. "I know it's a shock, but these things can work out for the best."

"For whom?" replied Charlie.

"For us!"

"I'll meet you on Saturday morning, and you'd better have rock-solid proof of this pregnancy. The tea rooms on the seafront. Eleven a.m."

"See you then," Delores said brightly.

Charlie set down the receiver, shaking. He reached for his cigarettes, slammed the packed down, and lit up. Inhaling deeply, he leaned back in the chair. At that moment, the door opened, and Mark entered the room enthusiastically.

"Hey, my week was awesome, how about yours?" Seeing Charlie's serious face, he stood back. "What's with you and the cigarette? You haven't finished with Sophie, have you? She's the best."

"No, I haven't finished with Sophie," Charlie sighed.

"What's up, mate? Want to talk?"

"Ok, but it stays with you, right? This doesn't go out of this room."

"God's honour," replied Mark as he pulled up a chair.

Charlie looked at Mark, taking a deep drag on his cigarette. "I won't beat about the bush. I'm going to be a father."

"Well, congratulations!" Mark exclaimed. "Finally. I know you and Sophie have been trying. When's the baby due?"

There was a deathly silence, and Charlie took a deep breath. "I don't know all the details," he replied.

"What?"

"It's not Sophie," Charlie whispered.

Mark's hand went to his mouth. "What the fuck? How did that happen? And with who, Charlie? You're totally in love with Sophie."

"I was drunk after Grandma's party, and Delores tricked me. She pretended to be Sophie."

"Delores!" shouted Mark. "The tall gorky girl with short hair and a pointy nose? You must have been well gone, mate. What were you thinking?" he laughed.

"Look, Mark, this is not a fucking joke. She tells me she's pregnant and it's mine. I'm meeting her on Saturday to talk things over, and I've asked her for proof."

"Good luck with that one," replied Mark. "What are you going to tell Sophie? She's going to be heartbroken."

"You don't have to tell me that," snapped Charlie. "Look, I'm saying nothing until I've meet with Delores." At that moment, the phone rang.

"I got it!" cried Sophie. "I got my first staff nurse job!"

"Well done," answered Charlie. "You are going to be the best, and we'll celebrate. I must go and see Grandma on Saturday. Paperwork she wants me to help her with."

"Ok, see you on Sunday? I love you," she said.

"I, I love you too," answered Charlie, trying to contain his emotions.

# 16

## Where Is the Proof?

Delores sat in a window seat, looking out at the large, angry waves crashing on the beach. Rain pounded on the window. Nervously, she pulled out the scan and blood results confirming her pregnancy.

Charlie walked into the coffee shop and sat down opposite her in a business-like manner. "Ok, what is all this nonsense?" he began.

"Let's start with the proof you asked for," she replied and pulled put the scan and blood results. Charlie snatched them out of her hand and began to inspect the information.

"So, you're pregnant. How do I know it's mine?"

"Work it out, Einstein. The dates fit perfectly, and I certainly didn't have sex with anyone else. I'll have a paternity test, if you insist."

Charlie sat back and sighed. "So, what do you want, money to disappear?"

"No," replied Delores, shocked. "I want us to be a family."

"No, that is just not going to happen. I will support you, and that's it."

"Ok, have it your way," she responded angrily. "I can take care of myself, and I'm sure your grandma will be a wonderful support." She then reached into her handbag to get a tissue, pretending to be tearful.

"Oh, stop that," said Charlie. "We'll work something out, ok, just don't get emotional."

"Really?" pleaded Delores. "What shall we do?"

"I don't know. I need some space, some time to think," replied Charlie.

"Don't leave it too long. I'll start to show soon. The girls at work have already noticed my morning sickness," Delores retorted.

"I'll call you on Monday, but please in the meantime keep this under your hat," responded Charlie.

"Very well," Delores replied with confidence. "Call me on Monday," and she passed him her business card. "What will you tell Sophie?"

"Leave her out of this," he snapped. He then stood up. "Make sure you have lunch," he said and put money on the table before leaving.

# 17

# The Unbearable Decision

Back home, Charlie walked towards the phone. After a sleepless night, coupled with endless cigarettes and glasses of wine, he was forced to make an agonising decision. In his heart, he wanted to stay with Sophie. However, he knew that Delores would make sure Sophie found out about the baby and flaunt the fact that it was his. How would Sophie ever trust him again? Grandma would be totally unforgiving and haunt him with her anger, not to mention disinheriting him and instead giving everything to Delores. There was also the baby to consider. How could he walk away from his responsibilities as a father? He couldn't put this off any longer. Feeling broken, he dialled Sophie's number. He had no choice. Delores had him in a corner.

"Hello?"

"Hi Sophie," Charlie answered, voice flat.

Sensing something amiss, Sophie felt panicked. "What's wrong? Are you ill? Do you want me to come over?"

"No, it's just… I don't know how I feel anymore. I will always love you and our time in Paris. But I think we need a break."

"What?" cried Sophie. "I thought—" Her eyes were filling with tears as she took a seat and placed a hand on her chest, trying cope with the pain and immense emotion. "Is, is it because I didn't get pregnant?" she sobbed. "I have that appointment booked."

"No, no, it's nothing to do with that, and promise me you will keep that appointment," replied Charlie, trying desperately not to become emotional himself. "You are wonderful, and someone someday will be so lucky."

"You're finishing with me, then," she sobbed, now blinded by tears.

"Sophie, please, I adore you. I just cannot be in a relationship right now."

"Is there someone else?" she whispered.

Charlie closed his eyes and remained silent momentarily, finding Sophie's distress more than he could bear. "I can't talk anymore, Sophie. Please remember the good times we had together and hold onto them. I will, forever."

"Then why are you ending this?" she screamed. "Can I see you just one more time?"

"No," he whispered. "It's just better this way. Look, I'm moving out of the flat. You can pick up your things and your books. Mark will still be here."

Sophie was now sobbing uncontrollably.

"Look, I know you're devasted. Believe it or not, so am I," said Charlie. "Please take care of yourself. You are a wonderful nurse, and I just know you'll get into midwifery school. Goodbye, Soph. Even though we won't be together, you will always remain in my heart and my thoughts."

Charlie set down the receiver, not believing what he had just done. In desperation, he picked up a cushion and threw it at the wall. A nearby shelf shook, and his prized photos of the trip to Paris fell to the floor, glass shattering. "No, no, I did not mean that to happen!" he cried desperately, gathering them up. He went to the fridge and poured a large glass of wine, shaking with emotion. "Well, Delores, I hope you're happy now!" he shouted.

Sophie had placed the receiver down, hardly able to breathe. For a moment, she bowed her head into her hands and thought she might faint.

A moment later, there was a tap on the door of the telephone booth. The friendly warden said, "Are you alright, dear? I heard your sobbing from the corridor."

"Oh, sorry," replied Sophie, rubbing her eyes and trying to pull herself together. "I just had some bad news."

"I'm sorry to hear that. Boyfriend trouble, is it?" she said, shaking her head sympathetically and handing Sophie a box of tissues. "They're not worth tears, love, mark my words."

Overcome with emotion, Sophie took the tissues. "Thank you. I need to go to my room."

"Yes, go and have a nice cup of tea. You'll feel much better soon."

Sophie ran up the stairs, not stopping to speak with anyone. As she reached her door, she took her pen and wrote on the board: DO NOT DISTURB. Then she lurched in and slammed the door behind her. Exhausted with tears and emotion, she lay on the bed, staring up at the ceiling. Finally, she closed her eyes and tried telling herself it was all a horrible nightmare, a mistake. Charlie would call her again, she was sure.

# 18

## Glad Tidings

Charlie sat in the hotel lobby with Delores, trying to look happy. They had decided to announce their engagement as soon as possible and get the wedding arrangements under way. Grandma and Mrs. Jackson arrived at the restaurant on time.

Greeting them both and unable to contain her excitement, Delores waved and called her over. "Let's take a seat, the menu looks wonderful."

"So, to what do we owe this pleasure?" Grandma asked once they were all seated, intrigued that she and Mrs. Jackson had been invited to lunch.

Before Charlie had a chance to answer, Delores blurted, "Well, we have some wonderful news for you, Grandma. Charlie and I are engaged!" she exclaimed, proceeding to hold out her left hand and show off her diamond ring.

Grandma put down the menu and clapped her hands. "Oh my goodness, that is wonderful news!" She then turned to the waiter. "A bottle of champagne, please. Congratulations to you both," she then said.

Charlie forced a smile. "Thank you, Grandma."

The waiter then approached the table with the champagne and four glass and began pouring, handing one to Grandma and then Delores. As Delores put out her hand, Charlie reached forward. "Mrs. Jackson can have this one. You wanted an orange juice, didn't you?"

"Don't be ridiculous," scolded Grandma. "Delores wants champagne to celebrate."

"Actually, Grandma, Charlie is right. I can't drink now."

"Why dear, what's wrong?"

"Well—"

This time, Charlie interrupted. "Grandma, Delores is going to have a baby."

Mrs. Jackson gasped, and bubbles went up her nose. She began to cough.

"I see," said Grandma. "Having a baby before getting married is the modern way. However, I am delighted for you both, and I assume that you'll be getting married as soon as possible."

"Yes," replied Delores. "I have made some provisional bookings. I thought I could pop round to your house to get your opinions. I was going to recruit Mrs. Jackson, too. I've met with some wedding planners, but really, they are so tiresome."

Charlie rolled his eyes as he sipped his champagne. He just wanted to get this wedding over with the minimum of fuss.

# 19

## Memories

Sophie stood outside the familiar door of the flat. Her heart fluttered. Perhaps he was there. Perhaps he was going to open the door and sweep her up like the first time she had visited him. She pressed the buzzer in anticipation.

A moment later, Mark opened the door, giving a sympathetic smile. "Hi, Sophie, come in. Charlie said you would be dropping by to..." He hesitated as he saw the pain in Sophie's normally cheerful face. "To pick up some stuff."

"Yes, thank you," she replied. As Sophie walked into the apartment, she noticed a distinct difference. The place seemed empty, lacking many of the familiar ornaments and belongings that had usually been there.

"Coffee?" called Mark. "It's cold out there. How's the new job?"

"Fine, I love it," responded Sophie, trying to sound normal. As she passed Charlie's bedroom, the door was open, and it was bare, with just a plain sheet over the bed. "Bones has moved out as well then," she joked.

"Yes," chuckled Mark awkwardly.

Sophie looked over at a small box neatly packed with the textbooks she had brought over for revision. On the top was an envelope with "Photos" printed on the front.

"He asked me to make sure you got these." Mark handed it to her. "Look I am so, so sorry that it didn't work out." He then passed her a cup of coffee. "Sit down and at least have a warm drink before you go."

Sophie looked over at Mark, sensing there was something he wanted to tell her. She wrapped her hands around the welcome drink and made eye contact with Mark. "What the hell happened?" she asked fighting back her emotions.

"It's not for me to…" He stopped. "Actually, I will tell you. Charlie loved you very much, and as far as I know, he still does."

"Then what?" Sophie asked, feeling confused but hopeful.

"Well, something happened, Sophie. I shouldn't be telling you this. There was someone else, a stupid trick, and now, now he's paying for it and they're getting married. I am so sorry. The worst thing is I have to be the best man."

"This is so baffling!" said Sophie. "Have you met her, then?" she asked.

"Um, yes," Mark replied hesitantly. He placed his coffee by the sink and turned towards her. "You have too."

Sophie frowned. "I've met her. Where?" Her mind raced, trying to think of who he might mean.

"It's Delores," Mark whispered.

"Delores!" Sophie exclaimed. "He doesn't love Delores!"

"Exactly," replied Mark.

"I don't believe it," whispered Sophie. "He's marrying Delores. I assume they're not going to live in Poplar."

"No," laughed Mark. "They got a house near his grandma. A really nice place, with three bedrooms. Oh God, how do I break this to you. I'm sure you'd find out anyway. He's marrying Delores because she's pregnant."

Sophie felt stunned, not even knowing how to answer. "Well, thanks for letting me know. I'll go now."

"If you love him, Sophie, let him go," Mark pleaded. "Look, at least take the photos. You will always have Paris. He raved about it for weeks."

"It's ok," she answered and placed the envelope on the table. "Enjoy being best man. Give my love to the bride and groom."

Sophie picked up the box and left the flat, feeling hurt and disorientated. She walked into the lift and pressed the button for the ground floor.

"Well," she thought, "I've been invited to a party, and God am I going to enjoy myself."

As Mark began to clear the coffee cups from the table, he spotted another envelope, under the table. It must have fallen and fluttered to the floor. Picking it up, Mark saw it was addressed to Sophie. The handwriting was Charlie's. Hoping he could catch up with her, Mark ran to the door and called Sophie's name, but it was too late. As he reached the elevator, he saw she had already gone. Feeling upset, he went back into the flat and put the letter into his jacket. He would return it to Charlie next time they saw each other, so he could send it to her.

Dear Sophie,

I am writing this letter because I wanted to tell you how much I am hurting and to explain why I had to say goodbye. Firstly, I didn't end our relationship because I don't love you, I ended it because I do and wanted to save you from any further heartache.

The night of my grandmother's party, when you were still at the hospital, Delores came to our room and cunningly tricked me into thinking it was you. In the morning, I was in disbelief and panicked that you were not with me. Two months later, Delores informed me that she was pregnant. I wanted to tell you myself, but I didn't have the courage. It was cowardly of me, and I am deeply ashamed now. I don't stand with Delores, but I do stand with the baby and hope to be a good father.

Starting a family was our dream, and I will never forget the wonderful time we spent together and the plans that we made. Our time in Paris was magical, and I will hold onto those memories forever.

You are a wonderful nurse, and I just know that your ambition to enter midwifery will be realized. I hope you will find someone who loves you as much as I do, and they bring you happiness.

Please forgive me.

Charlie

80

# 20

## The Rescue

Sophie sat applying her make-up and brushing her hair when there was a knock on the door. She opened it to see Helena and Joanna all dressed up, eager to take Sophie out and make sure she enjoyed herself at the party.

"You ready then?" asked Joanna enthusiastically.

"Just about. I just need to finish my make-up."

"Well, you look very nice," said Helena in her ladylike manner. "Are you ok?" she asked sympathetically.

"If you mean am I over him, no, but I am determined to carry on. Everyone keeps telling me the hurt gets less with time."

Jo sat on the bed and was applying her own lipstick when she stopped and rolled her eyes. "Look, Soph, forget him, he's an idiot. Men like him aren't for relationships. They're just for exercise. Now come on, let's go."

"Jo, really!" replied Helena in a shocked manner. Although Sophie felt sad, she couldn't help but find her friend's remark comical and began to laugh.

As Sophie entered the club, there was a joyful atmosphere, with people talking and laughing in groups and loud music playing. Some already on the small, central dance floor were moving to the music blasting from a jukebox.

Joanna's eyes lit up as she spotted a few of the soldiers from the nearby barracks, leaning against the bar.

"I'll get the first round," she said. "Why don't you two find some seats."

Sophie and Helena sat at a corner table and were amused at Joanna's interactions with the soldiers. Joanna came back to the table holding the arm of one and with another young soldier carrying a tray of drinks.

"Sophie, Helena, this is Chris and his friend Andy."

Andy set down the drinks and shook hands with Sophie and Helena. "Nice party. Congrats on graduating."

"Thanks," said Sophie. I've applied for midwifery training and hopefully will start in May."

"Oh wow," he replied. "Nice one."

As a certain song came on, Chris grabbed Joanna and they headed for the dance floor.

"Yeah, I love this song," said Andy, laughing. "Want to dance?"

"Why not?" she replied, thinking he was nice enough.

As the disco turned into a slow dance, Andy went to put his arm around her. Sophie frowned and pushed him away.

"I'm just going to the ladies' room."

As she left the dance floor, she looked for her friends. Joanna was enjoying herself, and Helena had already left, as she was scheduled to work a day shift the following day.

Heading for the door, Sophie suddenly felt a tug on her arm and turned around. Andy smiled. "Leaving so soon?" he said, annoyed by Sophie's rejection of his advances. "Not good enough, eh?"

"No, it's not that. I just want to go."

"Somewhere more fun," he interrupted and began to drag her through the doorway. "My mate will drive us."

"No," she cried, pulling back, but he was much stronger.

"Oy, I think the lady said no," came a voice from behind her.

Sophie tried to turn round but felt Andy tighten the grip on her wrist.

"What's it got to do with you, mate? You know what, why don't you turn around and go about your business? We're just leaving."

To her relief, she recognised the other man, whom she knew as Jeff, the friendly security guard stationed on reception at the hospital where she worked. Sophie looked at Jeff with desperation.

"No, why don't you let her go and disappear," he answered.

Andy laughed. "Like you're going to make me."

"If you insist," replied Jeff and gave Andy a hard shove to his shoulder, allowing Sophie to break free.

Andy stepped forward and was about to throw a punch when one of his friends appeared. "Leave it, Andy, it's not worth it. Let's get back to the barracks."

"Good advice," said Jeff, standing a little in front of her.

Andy swung around and glared at Sophie. "You know what, no wonder your boyfriend ditched you. Jo told me the story and hoped I could cheer you up. You need to loosen up. A long night with a good man, that's what you need."

"I said leave it, Andy," his friend shouted as he directed him towards the door. He then turned towards Sophie. "Sorry," he muttered.

Sophie stood in shock, shaking, try to process what had just happened.

"Thank you so much," she whispered, turning towards Jeff.

"It's ok, you're safe now. I'll walk you back to the nurses' home. Oh no, you're shaking," Jeff commented with concern. "Let me get your coat for you."

Jeff was a complete gentleman, and after retrieving her coat from the coat check, he assisted Sophie with putting it on. "I'll need to let my friend know," she replied.

Jeff gave a discreet cough. "I think she's busy," he replied, glancing over to Jo and her new boyfriend snogging in the corner.

"I see," she said, nodding.

As they reached the door to the nurses' accommodation, Jeff paused.

Sophie turned, wishing to express her gratitude. "Thanks again."

"No problem. You meet idiots like him all the time," Jeff replied. "Look, take care of yourself. None of my business, but sorry to hear about your boyfriend." Tears began to run down Sophie's cheeks as she turned the key in the door. "Oh no, I didn't mean—"

"It's ok," replied Sophie.

"Look, if ever you need a friend, just someone to talk to, I am all ears. I play footie every Sunday, mad about the game. If you want to drop by and cheer on the team, you'd be more than welcome. I play for the Poplar Panthers. It's just a local team, but we've recruited some very promising players. The pitch is near Victoria Park."

"Thanks," replied Sophie. "You're very kind."

# 21

## The Game

Sophie woke up and drew back the curtains. Had last night really happened? Not wanting to stay in her room, she decided to watch Jeff play footie. Anticipating he might want a warm drink and a snack, she made a flask of coffee and tucked a packet of her favourite ginger biscuits in her bag, then got dressed, grabbed her coat and scarf, and headed out the door.

As she walked down by the canal and towards the park, she wondered how she could thank Jeff. God knows what would have happened if he hadn't intervened. As she reached the playing field, she saw the players and heard the familiar sound of a whistle. Jeff was in possession of the ball and skilfully outplaying his opponents, making his way towards the goal. Sophie kept her distance, not wanting to cause any distraction. Suddenly, there was a massive cheer from the crowd as Jeff scored, giving his team the winning goal. Sophie couldn't help but join in the celebration, jumping up and down. "Way to go, Jeff!"

As the players came off the field, Jeff spotted Sophie and came jogging over.

"Hi, you made it, then!"

"Um, yes," she replied. "I thought you might want some coffee. Oh, and I brought some of these," she said, pulling out the packet of ginger biscuits.

"Girl, they are just my favourite." He beamed. "Let's take a seat," and he pointed to a little park bench.

Sophie sat and carefully poured the coffee into a cup, then handed it to him. Jeff took a seat, keeping a respectful distance on the bench. "Here's to the beautiful game," said Sophie. "Today, Poplar, tomorrow, Wembley."

Jeff chuckled. "Yeah, right. Thanks for this," he nodded at the coffee.

"You're welcome. That's what a friend is for."

"Yes," replied Jeff. "It's good to have friends."

Sophie smiled, glad that boundaries seemed set. This was a friendship, not a budding relationship.

# 22

## Lilly's Birth

It was 2 a.m. in the private wing at St Thomas's Hospital. After a very short and uncomplicated labour, Delores was sitting up in bed, sipping Earl Grey tea and munching on freshly made pancakes. Charlie sat in the chair beside her, gazing adoringly at his new baby daughter. If only this had been his and Sophie's moment. Not a day went by that he didn't think about her.

"Will she do?" asked Delores. "Do you think Lilly will suit her as a name?"

"Yes," said Charlie. "It's a beautiful name. She looks like she's hungry. Are you going to feed her?"

Delores peeked over and considered. "Yes, she does. Now," she said, looking at the clock, "where is the maternity nurse? The midwife told me she would call her, then went to warm some formula."

"Delores, you know breast feeding is better."

"Yes, I know. I will. I mean, perhaps. I'm just a bit tired right now.

"Who is the maternity nurse?" Charlie asked.

"Oh, didn't I mention? Mrs. Jackson is taking care of this."

"Mrs. Jackson isn't a maternity nurse." replied Charlie.

"No, but she recommended one. Linda someone or other. Lots of experience."

There was a knock at the door, and the midwife appeared, followed by a middle-aged lady in a bright pink set of scrubs.

"Hello," she said, "I'm Linda, maternity nurse. We spoke on the phone." She had a mild Scottish accent. "Congratulations to you both. Now, I'll see to Miss Lilly and give her a feed, and you can get some rest."

"Oh, you're a darling," replied Delores. "Thank you."

Charlie reluctantly gave the baby to Linda and looked at Delores in a totally disapproving manner.

"Could you pass me that menu?" Delores asked. "I need to build myself up."

# 23

# Letter of Acceptance

Sophie ran down the stairs to check the mail slot. The decision letter was due to arrive any day. Sure enough, a white envelope with the Royal London Hospital School of Midwifery emblem already sat waiting for her as the warden continued sorting the post.

Sophie held it in her hand, looking at the envelope in anticipation. Then, unable to contain her excitement, she ripped it open and began to read:

> *Dear Miss Thomas,*
> *We are pleased to inform you that your application to the*
> *Royal London School of Midwifery has been successful.*

"Yes!" cried Sophie, elated.

"You got in, then?" came a familiar voice behind her. Helena stretched her arms out to embrace her friend at the good news, so happy that something nice had finally happened.

"I can't wait," cried Sophie. The warden approached them and passed her another envelope. Sophie saw it was from the clinic she had been referred to by her GP.

"Thank you," she said, tucking it into a pocket to open later.

# 24

## Devastating News

Sophie entered her family doctor's office, dreading the appointment. She had undergone numerous tests in the past few weeks. There had never been any fertility problems within her family. In fact, her sister and cousins had conceived easily and had straightforward pregnancies. Hoping to get some answers, she nervously knocked on the door and heard, "Come in."

As she entered the door to his office, she knew almost immediately it wasn't going to be good news.

Dr. Cruz gave Sophie a sorrowful look as he gestured for her to take a seat.

"Well," he began, "I'm glad you made your appointment today. We do have some results back." He rustled through her chart to view the blood test results, then looked up and leaned forward.

"Sophie, I am so sorry to tell you that your blood tests show you are suffering from a condition known as premature ovarian failure."

Sophie froze in her chair. Surely this was a horrible nightmare, and she would wake up any moment. But as the doctor continued, she knew it was all too real.

"I know you're a nurse. Are you familiar with this condition?"

"I've heard of it," whispered Sophie, trying to fight the tears already welling up and trickling down her cheek.

The doctor passed her a box of tissues and waited a moment before continuing. "There are several causes. However, it seems in your case it is a result of a genetic condition called Turner syndrome."

"So, I will never be able to have children?" Sophie sobbed.

"Well, medicine and science are continually evolving. IVF is still very new, but I have heard of a clinic in London that uses a technique with donated eggs. I will start you on some hormone replacement therapy and arrange some genetic counselling." He scribbled a prescription on his pad, then tore it off and handed it to her.

"And that's it?"

"Unfortunately, yes," he replied. "Again, I am so sorry. There may be a support group you could connect with."

"A support group," Sophie responded, unintentionally raising her voice in distress. "No, I don't want a support group. I wanted to have a baby." Unable to withstand any more, Sophie stood up and left the room. Heading through the medical building doors, it was like the whole world stood still. She had lost Charlie. And now, this. It just seemed so surreal. Feeling shaken, Sophie sat down on a little bench and discreetly wiped away what seemed to be an endless river of tears. Trying to process the devastating news, she was determined it would not stop her dream of becoming a midwife and carry on with other life ambitions. Although she might not become a mother, she took comfort in the fact that she was a doting aunty, and pulled out a photo she had in her purse. It was a happy picture of herself with her nieces and nephews. Her new friendship with Jeff would also give her the strength to pull through and carry on.

# 25

## The Proposal

Sophie stood on the sidelines of the football pitch. The wind was howling, and a sprinkle of snow had begun to fall. It didn't matter what the weather was doing, Jeff wouldn't miss his game. Sophie had found great comfort in Jeff's friendship and had complete admiration for the way he always acted the perfect gentleman.

"Hey you, Georgie Best," called Sophie.

Jeff waved and ran over.

"Look, I've been thinking," began Sophie.

"Oh no, that's dangerous," he joked.

She smiled at him affectionately, then said, "I have to work on Christmas Day. My sister is dropping me off some dinner, but I know it will be far too much. Would you like to come over and share some food? I'd like to thank you for being such a kind friend."

"If you're sure," said Jeff. "My brother and his family invited me over to Spain, but I don't really fancy it."

"Well, that's settled then," said Sophie, passing Jeff a mug of tea and some homemade cake.

—

Sophie rushed to her room, looking at her fob watch. Christmas Day had been busy, like any day on a medical ward. She was exhausted, but happy to be sharing her Christmas dinner with Jeff and looking forward to a relaxing glass of wine.

Sophie opened her curtains and peeked out. No snow, but a deep frost lay on the ground and covered the cars in the streets.

Attentively, Sophie laid a decorative cloth on a little table by the window, then added two Christmas crackers and a small decoration in the centre. On top of the little fridge, she had put a miniature Christmas tree, and the microwave had a tiny tinsel wreath attached to its door. Sophie's sister, as predicted, had brought lots of food, lovingly packed. Sophie was also looking forward to visiting her sister's house on Boxing Day, a family tradition which was full of fun.

Sophie had decided to buy Jeff some new football boots as a present and had decorated the box with his team's emblem.

There was a knock on the door. Jeff had arrived at 3 p.m. on the dot, as agreed, dressed in a smart sportswear jacket. Sophie opened the door. "Happy Christmas!"

"Happy Christmas," replied Jeff. The greeting was followed by a gentle hug and a peck on the cheek. He then handed Sophie a small poinsettia plant. "Oh, I love these, thank you!" exclaimed Sophie and proudly placed it on her windowsill.

As Sophie and Jeff finished their dinner, she reached for Jeff's present. "I hope you like this," she said, handing Jeff the box. "Thank you again for rescuing me that night."

"You're welcome," smiled Jeff. "You didn't have to."

"I know," giggled Sophie. "I hope they bring you luck and a place in the trials."

"I'll need it," laughed Jeff, carefully opening the box and beaming as he saw the new boots.

Jeff then reached into his jacket pocket. "Almost forgot," he coughed nervously. "I have a present for you, if you'll accept it."

"Oh," said Sophie, a little surprised as she gazed at a little box carefully wrapped with a red bow.

"Before you open it, I need to ask you something, and you can say no. I won't be offended."

'What is it?" whispered Sophie with concern.

"Well," said Jeff, "I am not a rich man. I probably never will be. But I wondered, if…if you would do me the honour of being my wife. Please, will you marry me?"

Sophie felt shocked and at first didn't know what to say. She sat down and looked into Jeff's eyes.

"Jeff, I am so flattered. You're such a nice guy, and you'll make a wonderful husband. But I can't. It just wouldn't be fair to you."

"Fair?" asked Jeff.

"Yes. Look, I don't go around talking about it, but I can't have children. There wouldn't be any babies."

"Babies," chuckled Jeff. "I thought you had invited me over for Christmas dinner and a glass of wine." Despite her seriousness, Sophie smiled at this. "I've asked you to marry me because I fell in love with *you*, not the idea of having children. Anyway," he joked, "you've met my cat Chester plenty of times. I don't think he'd be too happy about youngsters." At that, Sophie's heart melted. She opened the box and looked down at the diamond and ruby ring.

"So will you be my wife?" asked Jeff softly.

Sophie looked up at Jeff. "Yes," she exclaimed. "I will be your wife."

Jeff gently placed the ring on Sophie's finger, and they embraced.

At that moment, there was a knock at the door. Sophie opened it to find Joanna and Helena, rosy-cheeked from drinking wine and decorated with paper hats from Christmas crackers. "Happy Christmas!" they cried, then suddenly stopped as they saw Jeff at the table, smiling.

"Oh, guys," said Sophie, "Jeff is here, and, well, we just got engaged."

"Bloody hell," Jo shouted, "congratulations!"

# 26

## Every Picture Tells a Story
### November 2, 2009

Detective Jane Wyatt sat at her desk, carefully reviewing the coroner's report. As an experienced detective, she had been involved in many murder investigations. Turning the pages of the file, she felt strangely uneasy, almost haunted, as she looked at the pictures of Emily's lifeless body and the scene by the canal where she had been found. It was as if Emily was trying to tell her something. Jane shook her head gently and sighed.

"Ok, so what really happened, Emily? Where were you going?"

At that moment, there was a knock at the door. "Guv?"

"Yes, come in," she beckoned to Detective Sergeant Gary Brown.

"About the witch case," he began.

Jane's head snapped up, and she frowned sternly. "Are you referring to the investigation into Emily Robinson's death?"

Seeing her disapproval, he coughed and smiled. "Sorry. I didn't mean any disrespect. Well, we ran a general background. Apart from being involved in an animal rights protest, no trouble. According to family and friends, no current boyfriend, but she had a small group of friends who held pagan beliefs. When her parents discovered that she was experiencing so-called visions, they insisted she start seeing a psychiatrist. Overall, a well-liked girl. Oh, and she was adopted."

"So?" questioned Jane.

"Well, it turns out she was a twin," answered Gary.

Jane looked at her colleague in surprise. "Do we know anything about her twin?"

"They were identical, separated shortly after birth. Young single mother. The adoption was quickly arranged by her relatives. The other girl went to a couple who moved to the USA. Boston, I believe. Apparently, their marriage ended in divorce, leaving the girl troubled. When she reached eighteen, she moved away. Neither of her adoptive parents know where she is."

"Curious," murmured Jane. "Do we have a name?"

"Yes," replied Gary. "She goes by Alice. Is there anything interesting in the coroner's report?"

"Well," replied Jane, "the findings are consistent with accidental drowning. The only trauma was to her head. It looks like she tumbled and hit it on some broken railing.

At this stage of the inquiry, there is no evidence of any foul play. Unfortunately, there were no witnesses, and this part of the canal is not covered by CCTV."

Gary looked inquiringly at her. "So, it's open and shut, then."

"No, Gary, I want to find Emily's twin."

"How come, Guv?"

"Well," said Jane, picking up the photo of Emily, "something in this case is wrong. According to her friend who lives on one of the houseboats, Emily often walked the path by the canal, and she was aware of the broken railings. Also," she continued, "a bracelet with a Gemini emblem was found on the canal pathway. Her birthday was in late September. That makes her Libra. I want you to go back and speak with her family and any of her friends. See if any of them recognise this bracelet as belonging to Emily. Meanwhile, I'll contact the adoption agency and see what records can be retrieved. The other curious event," added Jane, "is that the office of a Dr. Ferguson, Emily's psychiatrist, was broken into shortly after Emily was found dead. The break-in is being treated as a separate matter at this time, but let's connect with that investigation."

"On it," replied Gary, nodding his head and exiting the office.

# 27

# The Demonstration

### November 4, 2009

Sophie felt both excited and empowered as she picked up her placard and joined her friends and colleagues outside the small midwifery unit under threat of closure. As the crowd grew, there were cries of "Save our unit, keep our midwives" and "Safe motherhood, no closures." After successfully completing her midwifery training, she had gained a position in a Midwifery-Led Unit in the heart of the East End. It served a diverse population and was cherished by the local community. Having worked so hard to establish the unit and knowing all the staff, Sophie wanted more than anything to stop the closure. Losing the unit would force patients to transfer care to the larger maternity units in and around London.

Charlie walked into the corridor leading from the mother-and-baby psychiatric unit following a consultation. He couldn't help but hear the commotion as he walked towards the main hospital entrance.

Heading for his car, he glanced over at a woman who seemed to be passively observing the demonstration. For a second, she looked at him and then suddenly hurried down an adjoining side road.

Just as Charlie reached his car, there was the sound of a loud bang, followed by a cloud of smoke. Then screams echoed as a motorcycle screeched and powered away from the crowd.

Charlie raced over to where a crowd was now encircling a young woman who lay motionless on the pavement. A nurse in uniform was kneeling beside her. "There's a pulse," she cried, but it's rapid, and her respirations are shallow."

Still wearing his white clinician's coat, Charlie knelt to assess the young woman and removed the scarf around her neck, then loosened her jacket collar. It had been two decades, but as he looked down, he knew it was Sophie; he froze as he saw the unmistakeable tattoo on her shoulder. "Sophie," he cried, "stay with us. The ambulance is on the way."

Sophie's eyelids flickered as she seemed to respond. Trying to keep her awake, he whispered into her ear, "Sophie it's me, it's Charlie. Do you remember Paris?"

"Can't forget," she whispered. Her condition then suddenly deteriorated.

There was a wail of sirens as the ambulance arrived and the paramedics descended. "We'll take over from here, doctor."

Charlie looked up to see a tall, well-built man racing towards the scene. "Sophie!" he screamed. "Sophie!"

"Are you a relative?" the paramedics asked.

"I'm her husband," Jeff shouted. "What's happened?" Charlie looked up at Jeff, who then said, "Who are you?"

Hesitating for a second, Charlie then replied, "I'm a doctor. I came to help."

After initially assessing and working on Sophie, the lead paramedic called, "Ok, let's go, let's go."

"I'll follow in the car," Jeff said. Turning to Charlie, he said, "Thank you, doctor."

"I am sorry I couldn't do more."

Charlie stood in disbelief as the ambulance raced away. For a moment, he had to convince himself that what had just happened was real, not a dream. Was this Emily's prediction? Had she really foreseen these events?

# 28

# Voicemail

Rachael entered the office, ready for her busy Monday morning ritual of unopened mail lying on her desk and the answering machine flashing furiously with messages. She poured herself a coffee and settled back in her chair as she pressed the play button.

"Charlie, Delores. Disaster, I couldn't get the caterers I wanted for Lilly's birthday party. Oh, and an old school friend is in town, so I'll be going away this weekend."

Rachael stifled a yawn, then frozen as the second message sent chills down her spine. After an initial silence, a woman's voice said, "Dr. Ferguson, I know your secret. Did you recognise her today?"

Rachael was used to unusual calls to the office. They were usually from a patient or a concerned relative. But this call was different and made her feel very uncomfortable. The caller number had been blocked, but Rachael felt she had heard that voice before.

As she tried to recall where, her attention turned to a courier who had appeared at the door. Strangely, it wasn't one of the usual couriers who delivered to the office. "For Dr. Ferguson," the courier said, placing a letter on her desk and swiftly turning to leave.

"Hang on," called Rachael, "what about signature?"

"Not necessary," called the courier, already halfway down the hall.

Rachael looked carefully at the envelope. Not the usual business stationery. On the front was simply handwritten "Confidential. For the Attention of Dr. Ferguson" with no return address. She didn't like the vibes she was feeling.

Rachael immediately rang the concierge at the front desk.

"Hi, George, did you see a courier leave just now? I didn't get the company name."

"Courier?" he replied. "I haven't seen one today. No one has passed by the desk, and I've been here all the time."

"Can you check your camera?" persisted Rachael.

"Sure," replied George.

There was a moment's silence. "Nope, no one here that I didn't see. Oh, hang on, yes, you're right. I was dealing with an enquiry. Looking at the footage, I can see what looks like a courier, a young woman, maybe. There is no recognisable logo. Just an orange jacket, motorbike helmet, and sunglasses. Seemed in a hurry and dashed out the door. Odd, not much sun around today. Is something wrong?"

"Well, she just seemed strange," replied Rachael.

Rachael placed the letter on Charlie's desk, knowing that he would be in to see his first patient in an hour's time.

When Charlie entered the office, Rachael called out, "Charlie, can I talk to you a moment?"

Seeing the unusual concern on her face, he walked in her office. "Sure, what's wrong?"

"Well, there was a voicemail message." Rachael pressed the play button. The first message from Delores began to play.

Charlie took a deep breath and looked up at the ceiling. "Oh, I am sure she'll get over it," he commented.

"Sorry, no, it's this next one that I need you to listen to," replied Rachael.

As she played the very short but haunting message, Charlie sat down. "No caller display, I assume?" he asked.

"No, afraid not. Does it make any sense to you?"

"Yes, sort of," sighed Charlie.

"There was also a letter for you, delivered by courier. I put it on your desk, along with the morning edition of the local paper. The hit-and-run was a terrible business.

"Yes," replied Charlie, "it was."

Charlie sat down in his office and looked at the envelope. As he opened it, a photograph of him kneeling by Sophie dropped out, and a note which read: "I think we're even now."

# 29

## The Affair

It was Friday afternoon, and Rachael had arranged to meet a friend in their favourite pub. As she had arrived early, Rachael settled into a booth and ordered a vodka soda with a dash of lime. As she studied the menu, a tall, elegantly dressed lady with dark bobbed hair and a designer handbag entered the bar arm-in-arm with a smartly dressed gentleman. He was impeccably groomed. Rachael had an eye for detail and noticed the Rolex watch on his wrist. *That must have cost a fortune*, she thought. As they sat in the booth next to hers, Rachael could not help but overhear their conversation.

"Steve, I just can't wait for us to be together this weekend. I thought this week would never end, and to top it all, I couldn't get the caterers for Lilly's birthday."

Steve gently clasped her hand. "Delores, darling, I have friends in the catering business. I'll sort it out for you. Look, when are you going to tell him? This has been going on long enough. I want you all to myself. You said yourself you're stuck in a loveless marriage."

"Soon," she replied. "I don't want Lilly to know until after her birthday. She adores her father, and I don't want her to become upset. Look, let's enjoy the time we have together now." There was a clink of glasses.

"To us," Steve whispered.

"To us," echoed Delores.

Rachael had never met her boss' wife but had spoken to her on the phone several times, and Delores wasn't a common name. Plus, his daughter's name was Lilly. It was Delores, with another man. Oh God, what should she do?

At that moment, Rachael's friend Hanna arrived and waved. "You ok?" she asked.

"Yes," replied Rachael. "Just a busy week."

As Delores and Steve got up to leave a bit later, Hanna looked over and whispered to Rachael, "They're a bit posh for this place, aren't they? Do you know them?"

"Not personally," answered Rachael. "Can I get you another drink?"

"Please. Fridays always call for a second gin and tonic," Hanna answered.

Rachael made her way to the bar and ordered her friend's drink. As she paid the bartender and picked up the glass, she felt a gentle tap on her shoulder. Turning around, she looked in surprise as she saw Charlie. He was dressed casually in jeans and a tee-shirt.

Rachael smiled, noticing the Motörhead logo. "I didn't know you were a fan," she smiled. "Would you like to join us for a bite?"

"Thanks, but I've already eaten. Been here some time, actually," he replied, looking over to the empty booth from which Delores and Steve had just departed.

"I see," said Rachael, feeling a little awkward.

"Exactly," responded Charlie, setting down his empty glass. "Look, have a great weekend, and I'll see you on Monday." With that, he waved and left the pub.

# 30

## I Will Return

Alice sat comfortably in the airport lounge, sipping her glass of wine. Glancing at the departure board, she saw that her flight to Boston wasn't for another two hours. The local news was playing. There was a blurred picture of a person on a motorbike and the scene outside the maternity unit.

The announcer began: "Police are looking for information leading to the identity of a motorcycle rider involved in a hit-and-run incident yesterday. The rider, apparently posing as a courier, drove into the protesters, hitting and seriously injuring midwife Sophie Thomas. Colleagues are devasted and cannot understand the vicious and unprovoked attack. Anyone with any information is asked to contact the police immediately."

Alice emptied her glass; the server approached and asked whether she would like another one. Looking at the screen, the server shook her head in disbelief. "Who would do such a thing? Terrible what you hear these days."

"Terrible," replied Alice, smiling enigmatically.

When the server reappeared with a second glass of wine, she said, "Here you go, love. I'm going off shift, but one of my colleagues will be glad to help you. Have a great flight, and hope to see you back in London soon."

"Indeed, you will," replied Alice, still smiling. "Indeed, you will."

# 31

## Frankly, My Dear

As the guests began to disperse, Lilly hugged her father with affection. "Thanks, Dad. It was the best birthday party ever," she whispered.

"I can't believe you're twenty-one and all grown up," replied Charlie. "Now, what time are you and your pals leaving for your trip to Amsterdam? I'll drop you at the airport, if you like."

"Oh, actually," Lilly answered with a slight blush, "Howard is going to drive."

"Howard?"

"Yes," replied Lily. "Howard is a student I met at university. He's studying journalism in the same program as me."

A young man then appeared, smiling and carrying Lilly's coat. "Hello, I'm Howard," he announced as he shook Charlie's hand. "I'm originally from Holland and will be showing our group around."

"Well, have a lovely time," smiled Charlie. Howard and Lilly then left. Charlie couldn't help but feel protective.

However, he knew she was an adult. And there was another piece of business he wanted to attend to.

Delores was busy clearing away plates and food when Charlie appeared in the doorway with an envelope in his hand.

"Delores, can we talk?" he asked.

Delores looked up and saw the serious look on his face. "Sure, is it about Howard? He's a good sort. I don't think we need to worry."

"No, it's not about Howard," Charlie replied with a sigh. "It's about us."

"Us?" chuckled Delores. "It's a long time since we talked about us."

"Actually, I have something for you," he responded.

"Oh my goodness," replied Delores in surprise, "but our anniversary isn't until next week."

"Well, I want you to have this now," he answered, placing the envelope in her hand.

Delores excitedly opened the envelope and unfolded the letter. As she began to read, she suddenly sat down and went pale. She looked up at Charlie and then yelled, "No, you can't do this. I don't want a divorce; I still have feelings for you."

"No," replied Charlie, "you only have feelings for yourself. Oh, and what's his name — Steve. You know, if you're going to have an affair, it might be an idea not to use our joint credit card. Which, by the way, is now cancelled."

Delores gasped as she suddenly realized she had paid for a hotel bar bill with the card.

"There will be a fair settlement, but the majority of the money Grandma left is going to Lilly, now she is twenty-one," Charlie continued in a business-like manner.

"Please, I still love you. It was just a silly fling," pleaded Delores. "My life will be ruined, ruined if you do this, I tell you."

"Now you know what it feels like, then," he responded.

"I'm just so devastated," Delores cried.

"Well, how does it go?" Charlie replied. "'Frankly, my dear, I don't give a damn.'"

Charlie then left the room, slamming the door. This wasn't the end. It was just the beginning.

In disbelief, Delores threw the divorce papers to one side and walked over to the area where the party drinks had been served. After pouring herself a large glass of wine, she took a gulp and then reached for her phone to text Steve.

> Steve, I told him I am leaving. We're getting a divorce! At last, we can be together. Let's meet tomorrow.

A few minutes later, her phone pinged. Delores snatched it up in excitement and began to read.

Darling, glad you made that decision. But Amanda returned with the children last night and wants to give our marriage another go. It was great while it lasted. Ciao babe

Steve x

# Epilogue

Although the memory of Sophie and their time in Paris never left him, Charlie began a new chapter in his life. Haunted by Emily's death, he accepted the offer of a partnership in a new private practice. Rachael remained at his side and was promoted to practice manager.

Delores joined an exclusive dating agency and met Cameron, a wealthy stockbroker. Fun was to be had in the emerging dotcom world.

Meanwhile, Lilly became an investigative journalist. Together with Howard, they produced their own magazine, *Beyond Reason*, specializing in strange and paranormal stories.

Detective Jane Wyatt continued with her investigation into Emily's death, digging deeper to unravel the mystery and discovering more clues leading to Alice.

After Grandma passed away, the now elderly Mrs. Jackson made her own last will and testament, revealing a secret from her past in the hope of gaining peace of mind. But her disclosure had some unexpected consequences.

Sophie recovered from her injuries and returned to her midwifery career. However, when midwifery manager Louise Tupper introduced Sophie to a new student midwife, something seemed strange. Sophie felt an overwhelming sense of déjà vu...

POPLAR MYSTERIES

# Join Me on a Special Journey!

First, I hope you have enjoyed reading my first book as much as I enjoyed writing it. Are you curious to know what happened to Sophie? Were you left wondering whether and how Alice will return? Join me as I take you back in time to May 1990 and follow Sophie as she enters the amazing world of midwifery. It is her dream, her calling. Sophie's journey from student to registered midwife is filled with the joy of witnessing the miracle of birth and bringing new life into the world. However, she soon discovers that the tide of normality can change in a heartbeat, filling some days with tears, sadness, and frustration. Every encounter tells a different story and creates incredible memories. As Sophie walks through the doors of a busy delivery suite, what lies on the other side is often a tale of the unexpected. *From Here to Maternity* is her story.

A sneak peek at the first chapter of
**_From Here to Maternity_**

# 1

# Between Two Worlds

Sophie opened her eyes to the sound of sirens. The air was thick with smoke and the sound of screams. Familiar voices were calling her name. She looked around, bewildered, seeing familiar faces. But everything seemed different. And when she tried to move, her body was heavy and unresponsive. Panic overwhelmed her, as she remembered a motorcycle careening towards the cluster of protestors. *I must have been hit*, she thought. Her head spun and throbbed, and her chest shrieked from injuries.

Then there was a sudden calm and silence, as if time and place had lurched to a halt. Sophie's attention was drawn to a young woman sitting beside her. The long, dark hair and mystical eyes seemed familiar.

"Do I know you?" she whispered. "You're Emily, aren't you? The girl I saw in the newspaper."

"I am," the woman replied with a kindly smile. She then reached out to hold Sophie's weak, cold hand.

"How are you here? You're dead," replied Sophie.

"I am here to help you. You're right, I am not of this world. But it is not yet your time to leave. You have so much work yet to do and people who need you."

Sophie was puzzled. What work, and how could Emily help her? Before she could ask, she felt a sudden shift, as if leaving her body. Dozens of memories flashed before her, from childhood, youth, her student nurse days. The moment she met Charlie, the medical student she'd fallen in love with, and their time in Paris. Being cruelly jilted. Then came the kind and dedicated face of Jeff, the man who had rescued her and been there for her through thick and thin. Their wedding day. Her first delivery of a baby, with the gentle guidance of a kind midwifery sister mentor. Lifting the baby up towards the mother and hearing the first cries.

121

Then time recommenced, and Sophie seemed to rejoin her body. She turned to speak to Emily, but the apparition had disappeared. "No, don't go yet!" Sophie called.

"I'll be close by," came a soft whisper.

Sophie experienced a pang of sadness, but then her encounter with Emily's spirit filled her with strength and a will to keep living. Emily had shown Sophie that her life was meaningful and far from over. She had been given a second chance. An opportunity to make a difference, to help others and fulfil her purpose of bringing new life into the world. She took a deep breath as one of the paramedics said, "Sophie, can you hear me? We're right here. We're taking you to hospital."

Sophie gave a weak nod and tried to raise her hand in response. She had no idea what lay ahead, but one thing was certain: she was ready for anything.

# Acknowledgements

Writing this book has been a long and epic journey, and I never would have reached the finish line without the help and support of some very special people. It is only right to acknowledge and praise them for being there when I needed them and for believing in me and lifting my spirits when I felt my hopes were dashed.

First and foremost, I would like to acknowledge my friends and colleagues for cheering me on and for making me laugh and sometimes even blush. Your enthusiasm for my story ideas gave me the motivation to keep going, even when the writing process felt daunting.

However, no book would ever make it without the outstanding work of a professional editor, and I would like to give special thanks to Dania Sheldon. Your attention to detail and honest feedback made a significant difference in transforming my rough drafts into a polished manuscript. Thank you for your eternal patience and guidance and for working your magic. I feel privileged to have been a client.

I am grateful to the copyright owners who allowed me to use lyrics from a Motörhead song and to the Hal Leonard Corporation for issuing the licence.

I would also like to acknowledge the amazing work of Alex Hennig at Clear Design for the stunning cover design and all the illustrations, which help bring the book alive and engage readers.

Finally, I thank each and every one of my readers. I hope you enjoyed the story and will continue to travel with me on my journey as an author.

# About the Author

Melanie Ingram is a registered nurse and was a registered midwife in the United Kingdom. Moving to Vancouver, Canada in 2003, she began a new chapter of her life as a registered nurse in Labour and Delivery. She lives with her husband Jess, soulmate and a long-time fan of the band Hawkwind.

Although now retired from a long and eventful career in midwifery and perinatal nursing, Melanie has opened another door by authoring her first book. She derives inspiration not only from her passion for nursing and midwifery, but also from a fascination with the paranormal and a love of British detective series. Melanie enjoys combining these into an exciting story of surprise and suspense, with the added sparkle of romance and love, while taking readers back to an era close to her heart.

poplarmysteries@outlook.com

Printed in Great Britain
by Amazon

25863656R00078